VALLEY
of the 99

Center Point
Large Print

VALLEY of the 99

A WESTERN DUO

Wayne D. Overholser

CENTER POINT LARGE PRINT
THORNDIKE, MAINE

ST. JOHN THE BAPTIST PARISH LIBRARY
2920 NEW HIGHWAY 51
LAPLACE, LOUISIANA 70068

This Circle Ⓥ Western is published by
Center Point Large Print in the year 2020 in
co-operation with Golden West Literary Agency.

March 2020
First Edition

Printed in the United States of America
on permanent paper.
Set in 16-point Times New Roman type.

ISBN: 978-1-64358-541-3

The Library of Congress has cataloged this record
under Library of Congress Control Number: 2019954791

VALLEY
of the 99

TABLE OF CONTENTS

The Courage Builder

Dan Riley and the tall man in the hard hat and Prince Albert coat were the only passengers when the westbound stage rolled out of Vale. It was too dark to see the tall man clearly, but Riley noticed his lurching gait as he crossed the street from the saloon opposite the hotel. When he climbed into the stage and slumped in his corner, Riley caught the stench of cheap whiskey.

There was no talk that night. Riley didn't feel like talking because his recent failure weighed heavily on him. The tall man had even less interest in talking. He rolled around in his side of the seat, snoring drunkenly until the sun cleared the broken country to the east.

The stage made a breakfast stop at Stinking Water. Riley climbed down stiffly and grinned at the driver. "Your seats ain't much softer than the last time I rode with you." He went inside and was stirring his coffee when the tall man stumbled in.

"Coffee. Black and hot." The man cuffed back his hard hat and rubbed his forehead. He said more loudly: "Hurry it up. Coffee. Hot and black. I need about a gallon of it."

"Tuck your shirt tail in!" Ma O'Brien waddled across the room with the coffee pot. "What did you do to this *hombre*, Dan?"

11

"I beat him over the head with a club," Riley said.

The tall man gulped three cups of coffee, and then looked at Riley as if he saw him for the first time. "Are you the scoundrel who slugged me?"

Riley nodded and pointed at the coffee pot. "Mine's still too hot to drink. You must have an asbestos-lined gullet."

"It may be that my gullet has no lining at all." He produced a bottle of whiskey from his pocket and surveyed it with anticipation. "This, my friend, fixes everything. With its help, there is nothing too difficult for me, nothing too dangerous."

"You'd better take him with you to Harmony and buy him about ten quarts," Ma O'Brien said. "Then turn him loose on the syndicate crowd."

The tall man ignored her. " 'To climb steep hills requires the slowest pace at first.' " He replaced the bottle and nodded at Riley. "Shakespeare."

Ma O'Brien brought Riley's bacon and eggs. She asked: "You eating, Mister Shakespeare?"

The tall man drew back his bony shoulders. "Don't mix me up with William Shakespeare. I am Andrew Daniels, newspaper editor, philosopher, and writer. Perhaps I have a finer brain than Shakespeare. Only time and the judgment of unborn generations will decide."

Ma sniffed. "You won't have no brain if you

keep drowning it with whiskey. I asked if you wanted anything to eat?"

"Eating is for weaklings. I will take my breakfast in liquid form."

"So eating is for weaklings. Dan, you must be downright puny."

"No offense." Daniels held out his hand. "I presume we were fellow passengers."

"I presume we were, Daniels," Riley said, shaking the man's hand.

Daniels poured another cup of coffee. "You live in Harmony?"

"A couple of miles on the other side. The DR is my spread."

Daniels fingered his black string tie, bloodshot eyes making a cool study of Riley from his battered Stetson to his scuffed boots and back to his black-handled gun. He asked: "Would you say there were opportunities in Harmony for a newspaper man?"

"No. We have a weekly. The *Clarion*. It's edited by a gent named Ben Wheeler."

"Doubtless Wheeler could use another man to assist him with the editorials, to dissertate upon local problems and the beauties of the landscape."

"It takes more courage than a whiskey bottle can give a man to work on the *Clarion*." Riley rose and dropped a coin on the counter. "When you coming to town, Ma?"

"Me come to that volcano?" Ma shook her

head. "I'll wait till it blows its head off. Then I'll come to your burying."

"Won't be long," Riley said grimly, and swung toward the door.

Ma called: "Dan!" When he turned, she asked: "How long you been gone?"

"A month."

She took a long breath. "Why don't you sell and get out, Dan? You little fellers can't lick the syndicate."

"We aim to try. Anything happen?"

"Bill Buckner sold out. That night he was shot and killed in front of the Saddle Up."

Riley stood very still, his bronzed, high-boned face expressionless. He had counted on Bill Buckner to hold out. He asked: "Who did it?"

Ma spread her hands. "Nobody knows."

The stage driver shoved back his plate. "We're rolling," he announced.

Riley said—"So long, Ma,"—and went out ahead of the driver. He stopped, the slanting sunlight bright upon the trodden earth of the yard, and stood motionless, right hand at his side. He said: "Howdy, Flint."

The man he had called Flint had left his horse ground-hitched in front of the barn. He was a slender man with two guns buckled around his middle. His lips were thin and cruel and now held a small smile as if he had come to a chore he would relish.

14

"Howdy, Dan," Flint replied. "You should have stayed away."

"Looks like I got back just in time," Riley said. "Ma told me about Bill Buckner. That your work, Flint?"

"Hell, no. It was some of your bunch. Larry Clyde and the rest gave Bill hell for selling. Then they waited till it was dark . . . got him in the back with a Winchester bullet."

"I doubt it was that way," Riley said.

"Makes no never mind." The blue-eyed gunman motioned to the driver. "Start rolling, Fred."

"Wait a minute," Riley said. "Get out of the way or make your play, Flint."

Ma O'Brien called from a window. "No he won't, Dan. This here Greener is fixing to blow his head off."

"Stick to your coffee and biscuits, Ma," the gunman said easily. "You ain't rightly concerned in this business."

"Oh, yes, I am!" Ma cried. "I was here a long time before you and your damned syndicate moved in. I knowed Dan's pappy and his mother before him. I ain't gonna sit on my rump and let you kill him."

Flint's laugh was a soft taunting sound. "So you're using women to do your fighting, Riley."

"Put your Greener up, Ma!" Riley called.

"Not much I ain't. If you're real anxious to get shot, Dan, go find Black Mike Sand and plug

15

him. No sense risking your life on paid carrion like Flint Hogan."

"Some other time, Riley," Hogan said carelessly, and turned away. A moment later he was in the saddle and jogging westward.

Andrew Daniels had been standing in the doorway. Now he held out his bottle. "Have a drink, friend. You need it after that."

"Go to hell," Riley snapped, strode across the yard to the stage, and got in.

Daniels followed, still holding the bottle. "You're a brave man, Mister Riley. You and the woman you call Ma are the kind who made the West, held it against the Indians and outlaws until law became a fact."

"Shut up," Riley said.

Daniels was silent until the coach had wheeled out of the yard and started down the long Stinking Water grade. He stared at the bottle and then put it back into his pocket. "It is a false courage builder," he said somberly. "I have depended upon it too long, but I have a feeling I can lick it in Harmony, Mister Riley."

Riley looked at him sharply. He might have been fifty, possibly younger. His clothes had been expensive, but they were frayed and dirty now. Even the collar of his white linen shirt was soiled. His long-jawed face was fuzzy with stubble. Still there was a sort of dignity about him that overshadowed his untidy appearance.

"Harmony is no place for you," Riley said with some kindness.

"You have trouble," Daniels said. "I am a good writer, a better writer than you will commonly find working on a cow-town weekly. You need your side stated in ringing terms. I will do that. Your Harmony weekly will justly be called the *Clarion* for it will shout a clarion call for justice."

A pile of fancy words, Riley thought. He said: "Ben Wheeler is no fine writer, but he's honest and he's got guts. He'll do."

"Still he will need help," Daniels said stubbornly. "What is your trouble over?"

"Oh, shut up," Riley said testily.

"You are quite right to silence me," Daniels said after a moment. " 'Avoid a questioner, for he is also a tattler.' " He paused as if reaching into his mind for the author. "Horace," he announced proudly.

Riley opened an eye. "Your friend Horace was a smart *hombre*, Daniels. There are too many tattlers around Harmony."

Daniels leaned forward. "Believe me, Mister Riley, I can be of help. There are times when a pen is a greater weapon than a gun can ever be."

That, Riley knew, was true. Ben Wheeler, for all of his honesty and sound courage, did not have a flare for putting words together the way this whiskey-soaked Andrew Daniels did.

"You might go see Ben," Riley said finally. "I'll put in a word for you, but lay off the whiskey."

"Your trouble?"

"Nothing new in the cattle country," Riley said heavily. "A gent named Jeff York came up from California years ago with a herd, bought a chunk of swampland from the state, and started Skull south of Harmony Flat. My folks and some others came in from Kansas about the same time and settled the Flat. We're small outfits even now . . . do most of our work with maybe a hand or two. We got along all right until a year ago when York died. The syndicate bought Skull and the manager, Black Mike Sand, fetched in toughs like Flint and tried to make us sell. Now write about that, friend."

"I will," Daniels said earnestly. "I shall dip my pen in vitriol. I shall call on every man to stand on his rights and preserve his home."

The stage wheeled into Harmony shortly before noon, and the instant it reached the business block Dan Riley forgot Andrew Daniels. The sense of impending trouble was as tangible as a searing wind blowing in from the desert. It looked to Riley, in the one quick glance he gave the north side of the street, as if every member of the Combine was in town, all armed with Winchesters and Colts. On the other side, centering under the Saddle Up saloon's wooden

18

awning, was the syndicate crowd, Black Mike Sand in the middle.

Larry Clyde was the first to see Riley. He let out a squall and ran into the street, bawling: "How are you, Dan?" Others trailed behind to surround Riley the minute he stepped down.

"Did you get the money?" A dozen throats threw the question at him.

Riley stood beside the stage, a tall, bony man marked by his trade of horse and rope. He looked around the half-circle of men from red-headed Larry Clyde to John Blair at the end.

"No," he said.

A sigh went up from them as if they had known all the time it would be that way.

John Blair said: "It's all right, Dan. We'll make out."

"Yeah," Clyde said sourly. "We'll sell and get out."

Anger stirred in Riley. He regarded Clyde as his best friend. Their places lay together. They had swapped work, had drunk out of the same bottle, breathed the dust of the drag on the long drive south to the railroad at Winnemucca; they had slept beside the same campfire and stared at the sky and talked and made their dreams together. If there was a man who should have withheld judgment, it was Larry Clyde.

"Maybe you could have done better, Larry," Riley said.

"Now maybe I could." Clyde jerked a hand at Farr's Mercantile. "I ain't sure Farr's gonna carry us any longer. Even if he does, he ain't got enough grub on his shelves to see us through the winter. You was the last straw we was grabbing at."

"That's right," Blair said. "We kept hoping, Dan. There's still time to freight in supplies if we had money."

They were tired gaunt men who worked too hard. Some were older men who had come in to the Flat in the first wave of settlement. Others were younger, some married and some single, but there were two things they all had in common—a sense of failure and a growing desire to strike at the syndicate that was pressing them.

"I took the train from The Dalles to Portland," Riley said. "Came back on the boat. Grabbed a train to Boise. I've seen a hundred bankers all along the line. Talked my tongue loose at the hinges." He made a gesture of utter futility. "Same answer everywhere. Hard times all over the country."

"We'll make out," John Blair said calmly. He was old, white of hair and beard, a man that everyone, even Black Mike Sand, respected. "We used to throw everything together to live, Dan. Ate venison mostly. We can do it again."

"The hell we will," Clyde said bitterly. "Black Mike's in town. What are we waiting on?"

"None of that," Riley ordered.

The stage had rolled on down the street. Andrew Daniels waited in front of the hotel, a faded carpetbag on the walk at his feet. Across the dust strip the syndicate crew stood watching, Black Mike Sand's smile a challenge.

Clyde motioned to Sand. "Look at him. We've got to fight 'em or quit. If we quit, I'm selling and getting out of town before they plug me like they done Bill Buckner." He looked at Riley defiantly. "Then you'll be right up against Skull. What'll you do then?"

"I'll eat beef as long as I've got a cow. Then I'll eat jack rabbit." Riley's eyes met Clyde's rebellious ones. "You won't sell, Larry."

"I'll shoot me a syndicate man first!" Clyde shouted.

"Let's have a drink." Riley turned toward the Trail Dust saloon down the street, saw Daniels, and paused. "Get yourself a room. I'll take you over to the *Clarion* office after a while."

Riley went on, his friends falling in behind him as they always did. They listened to Clyde's outbursts, to John Blair's calm reasoning, but when there was something to be done, it was Dan Riley they turned to.

"I didn't think Buckner would sell," Riley said.

"It's the first break," Blair said. "There'll be others."

21

"I'm next," Clyde flung at Blair. "We're licked. I say Buckner's only mistake was not getting out of town."

"Aw, dry up," Riley said. "Black Mike wouldn't drill Buckner after he'd made the deal."

"Go on and have your drink," Clyde muttered. He wheeled away and stalked back toward the hotel.

"What's biting him?" Riley asked.

"Dunno," Blair said. "Been talking like that ever since you left."

They had reached the saloon, but Riley didn't go in, for Connie, Black Mike's daughter, had come out of the Mercantile, saw Riley, and waved to him. "Go ahead," he said, and went on toward Connie.

She was a small blue-eyed woman in her early twenties. Now, as always, she wore a blue shirt and Levi's, and a Stetson that dangled down her back from a chin strap, her chestnut hair shiny-bright under the noon-high sun.

"How are you, Dan?" Connie said in a friendly tone.

Riley lifted his hat. "Howdy," he said, a little surprised that Connie had waved, and more surprised that she had a friendly greeting for him. He had always liked her because she was honest and straightforward, but she was on the opposite side of the fence, a fact that set them worlds apart.

"I'm glad you're back, Dan," Connie said. "Clyde's been talking wild."

"Maybe he's got cause. I had no luck."

"Did you expect any?"

"A man can't live without hoping."

"Hoping isn't enough, Dan. The day of the small, independent rancher is gone."

He shook his head. "We got along until your syndicate moved in."

She slid her hands inside her waistband, troubled eyes on Riley. Again he wished, as he had many times, that things were different between them. She liked the country; she fitted here. More than once he had thought she was the kind who could move into his house and give it the home-like feeling that had been gone since his mother died. Then—and this, too, had happened many times— he felt a pang of conscience. Tana Marlowe expected to marry him, and he had let it drift that way, but he had never been sure. Never really sure.

There was this moment of silence between them. Then, more humbly than was her habit, Connie said: "Dan, we quarrel too much. Maybe it's because we look at everything from opposite sides, but we do agree on one thing. We don't want trouble."

He laughed shortly. "Only your idea for stopping it would be for us to sell out to the syndicate. Then your dad might even give me a job."

"He'd be glad to. He thinks a great deal of you."

"I suppose his way of showing it was to send Flint Hogan up to Ma O'Brien's place this morning to make me pull."

She gave a gasp, eyes filled with horror. "You don't think Dad did that?"

"Hogan works for Skull, and Mike runs the outfit, doesn't he?"

"He doesn't run it that way. And he didn't have Buckner shot." She motioned toward the *Clarion* office. "Wheeler was pretty hard on us in his last issue. Dad told him to pull in his spurs."

"So that's why everybody's in town."

She nodded. "I'm awfully glad you're back, Dan."

In a way it was a compliment, for she recognized his leadership and his common sense. He said, "Thanks. Now that I'm back, I'd better do something about it."

Wheeling, Riley strode across the street toward Black Mike Sand and the syndicate crew. It was entirely unexpected. He saw the Skull men stiffen and move forward along the walk. Some dropped hands to gun butts. Sand said something and they eased back, but they remained watchfully alert as Riley stopped in front of Sand.

"Howdy," Sand said.

Neither his tone nor his wide, full-jowled face told Riley anything. He slid his thumbs inside his waistband, similar to the stance Connie had taken a moment before. They were much alike, Connie and Black Mike, yet they were entirely different. It was a difference that was partly physical, for Connie was small and graceful and light complexioned, and Black Mike was thick-bodied with black hair and eyes and a wiry black beard that darkened half of his face and almost hid his mouth. There was another difference, too, an intangible thing in their natures that Riley had often sensed but had never been able to define.

"Howdy, Mike," Riley said. He took a quick look along the line of sullen faces, and brought his eyes back to Sand. "You boys after bear meat?"

"Not exactly," Sand said. "We rode in to give your friend Wheeler a fair warning about the future."

"Take twenty men to do that?"

"Might. Another friend of yours has been putting out some fight talk."

"Clyde?"

Sand nodded. "Look, Dan. I work for a syndicate. My orders are to expand, which same we aim to do, but not by murdering men. We'll give more than a fair price for your DR or any other outfit on the Flat. That don't call for fight talk, does it?"

Riley thought of mentioning Flint Hogan and decided against it. Hogan had long hated him. As

Connie had said, it might not have been Sand's idea.

Riley motioned to the Skull hands. "You've got your boys here at the same time my side's in town. That could add up to shooting trouble. We don't want that. You say you don't. Send 'em home."

Sand bristled. "The hell I will. Send your bunch home."

Riley shook his head. "I can't. You're the one who came in to threaten Wheeler."

Sand's wide jaw jutted forward. "We ain't moving till your Combine outfit does."

Here, Riley saw, was the big difference between Connie and her father. She had the capacity to compromise; Black Mike did not. Yet, when the chips were down, she would be as loyal to what she believed in as her father.

"We've got homes," Riley pressed. "It's different with you."

"No difference. I've got my orders."

"Carrying out orders from a boss a thousand miles away ain't the same as fighting for your home, Mike. I've been wondering who the syndicate is."

"As far as you're concerned, it's me," Sand said, a belligerent note creeping into his voice. "That's good enough."

"No, Mike. You're acting for the syndicate, but Skull ain't your home. That's the difference. If

26

there's trouble today, it'll be of your making."

Sand lifted his gaze to the second-story hotel windows. There was no softening of his granite face when he said: "All right." He swung to his men. "Pull out, boys. I'll be along later."

Riley stared at Sand. Nothing the Skull man could have done would have surprised him more. He had never known Sand to back up on anything once he had taken a stand, yet that was what he was doing now, and there seemed to be no reason for it.

The Skull riders obeyed at once and without question. Riley held his place in front of the Trail Dust until the men were gone. Then he said: "Thanks, Mike."

Sand smiled thinly. "You're a persuasive gent, Dan." His eyes probed Riley. "You like Connie?"

"We don't seem to get along," Riley said shortly, irritated by a question too baldly put.

"You're too damned good a man to waste yourself on the side you're on. Connie knows that. Maybe that's what's wrong." Sand reached into his pocket for a cigar. "You could go a long ways with the syndicate."

"No thanks," Riley said, and swung away from Sand into the street.

"Dan," called out Ben Wheeler, coming out of the *Clarion* office. "Just heard you were in town."

"Ain't been in long," Riley said, and started

down the center of the street toward the editor.

That was when the rifle cracked. Wheeler stopped as abruptly as if he'd slammed into an invisible wall, and went down. Riley stopped. His breath went out of him and for a moment his lungs refused to work. It was like a nightmare that a man knows is not true, yet he cannot waken and destroy the illusion of horrible reality.

The Harmony Flat ranchers poured out of the Trail Dust. Townsmen appeared in doorways, saw what had happened, and rushed toward the fallen man. Doc Medery came from his office on a high lope, bag in hand.

Riley shook off his paralysis and ran toward Wheeler, Black Mike Sand at his side, but it was Andrew Daniels who reached the editor first. He knelt in the dust, felt for his pulse, then rose and faced Riley.

"He's dead," Daniels said. "Was he your editor?"

Riley nodded.

The medico was there then, and the rest of the men formed a tight circle around Medery and the body. The doctor dropped to his knees, made his examination, and rose.

"He's dead all right. Shot through the heart."

Riley stared down at the still figure, thin and bent from years at the composing bench, faithfully reporting Harmony's births and weddings and deaths, voicing its hopes and prophesying a rosy future. When the syndicate had bought Skull and announced that it would buy every place on the Flat, Wheeler had thrown whatever weight he possessed against it. Because Wheeler had the only voice that could be raised against the syndicate, Black Mike Sand had been his enemy from the first.

Blair and the others must have thought of that the instant it occurred to Riley, for as soon as Wheeler's body was carried to the medico's back room, the Combine men faced Sand.

John Blair said: "We stood for Buckner's killing, Sand. We won't stand for this."

Watching from the hotel lobby, Connie ran into the street to stand beside her father, head held high. "What kind of men are you?" she cried. "He sends his crew home and then you accuse him of a killing he had nothing to do with."

"I don't know what kind of men we are," Blair said heavily. "Fools maybe, but we know there wasn't anybody else who wanted to silence the paper."

"He was on the street all the time with Riley," Connie flashed.

"He's got plenty of men to do the job," Blair said. "Better get off the street, ma'am."

For a moment Riley was sucked into a morass of indecision. Then Sand looked at him, smiling coldly.

"You got me to send my boys home to save trouble," he said. "Or was it to get my neck stretched?"

They were watching Riley, Connie and the rest, waiting to see what stand he took. Whatever his feelings were about Ben Wheeler, the fact remained that he was responsible for Black Mike Sand standing here alone.

"You aren't thinking of a neck stretching, are you, John?" Riley asked.

"That's exactly what I'm thinking about," Blair answered.

"No," Riley said. "We don't know where the shot came from or who fired it. We don't know that Sand had anything to do with it. So we'll wait."

Suddenly it seemed to Riley that he didn't know these men, men he had called friends, men who had followed his leadership. He saw in their bleak faces that they could stand no more. Hard times. A bank failure. Then the pressure from the syndicate.

"We've been waiting," Blair said tonelessly. "A lot of little things have happened since you left. We've been shot at. We've had haystacks burned. We've got warning notes in the mail telling us we'd better sell." He pointed a trembling finger at Sand. "What's our waiting got us but another dead man?"

"We had nothing to do with those things,"

Sand said. "We want your land and we'll take advantage of the hard times to get it, but that's as far as we go."

"You threatened Ben Wheeler," Blair said doggedly.

"I threatened him because he lied." Sand jerked a folded paper from his pocket and pointed at the headline:

SKULL MURDERS BUCKNER

"You and Connie had better leave, Mike." Riley pinned his gaze on Blair's face. "When we can prove that Sand was behind Ben's killing, I'll be the one to drop the loop over his head, but there'll be no necktie party until we get that proof."

"We'll never have a better chance to get a loop on his neck!" a man beside Blair shouted.

"Go on, Mike," Rilcy said.

Without a word Sand wheeled and strode to his horse.

Connie laid a hand on Riley's arm, murmuring: "Thanks, Dan. You'll never be sorry."

Then Connie was gone and for a moment Riley wasn't sure what Blair and the others would do. He looked at them, his face bone hard. Blair sucked in a long breath and dropped his gaze. Old habits of going Dan Riley's way had prevailed.

"You don't know it," Blair said irritably, "but

31

you're letting a pretty girl make a fool out of you."

"Two pretty girls make him worse than a fool!" Larry Clyde shouted in a high bitter voice. "You're forgetting Tana Marlowe. She owns stock in the syndicate."

A moment before Clyde had not been here. Now he stood in the fringe of the crowd, Winchester cradled in the crook of his arm.

Eyes swung to him, someone asking: "Where have you been?"

"Having a drink. I didn't know what had happened till just now."

He was a little drunk, Riley thought, on anger if not on whiskey. Clyde was trembling in his rage, and that seemed strange, for there was no reason for it. It was strange, too, that he knew Tana owned some syndicate stock, but the knowledge seemed to make no impression upon the others.

Riley said evenly: "We'll keep Tana out of this, Larry."

"Sure, and you'll keep Connie out of it." Clyde shook his fist at Riley. "You sashay all over the country and come back without a nickel. You tell us to wait. Hell, I say it's time we did some riding. Toward Skull."

Larry Clyde was not the man Riley had left a month ago. Again the feeling gripped Riley that this was a nightmare. It could not be happening. Larry had been his friend. Friend! A strange word for a man who was shaking a fist at him, so crazed by rage that he seemed beside himself.

"What we do with Skull won't change the shape we're in," Riley said.

Blair wiped sweat from his face. "When we stop to think," he commented, "we know that's true. Sand can't be to blame for our hard times."

"You're yellow!" Clyde bawled at both Riley and Blair. "I can't fight Skull alone. I'll sell and get out."

Clyde swung away to his horse, mounted, and quit town in a wild run. Stunned, they watched him go, and Riley felt that his world had fallen apart. Whatever happened now, the old warmth that had been between him and Larry Clyde was gone.

"What's the matter with Clyde?" a man asked.

"He's wanting to sell," Blair said, "and when he does, the syndicate will have a section of land in the middle of the Flat. They can do a lot of things with that." He took a long breath. "Well, Dan, we need an editor."

"I'll get your paper out," Andrew Daniels said from behind the group.

"What do you know about a paper?" Blair demanded.

"He came in on the stage with me," Riley said. "I don't know how good an editor he is, but we'll find out." He jerked his head at the *Clarion* office. "Come on, Daniels."

Andrew Daniels followed Riley across the street to the newspaper office. He stopped in the doorway and sucked in a deep breath, his gaze swinging around the composing room. There seemed to be no order anywhere, no neatness, just the jumble typical of country newspapers.

"This is something a man never forgets," Daniels said. "You can drink yourself into the gutter, you can hide behind all the excuses you can think of, you can swear to yourself a million times that you'll never come back, but if it's once been your world, you will come back and it will be like home."

He walked across the room to a type case, and sat down on the stool. Riley watched him, sensing a strength in the man that had been totally lacking that morning at Stinking Water.

"Is there a place to live here?" Daniels asked.

"Ben had a room in the back. I guess it would be all right to use it."

Daniels rose. " 'Eternal vigilance is the price of liberty.' " He cuffed back his hard hat, and added: "Jefferson."

"You saw what happened to Ben," Riley reminded him.

"Wheeler made the mistake of saying Skull killed Buckner. I kind of liked that man Sand. Ruthless, perhaps, but I think he'd be aboveboard. It strikes me you've got somebody else promoting trouble."

"There ain't nobody else."

"Maybe. Maybe not. But if there is, we'll smoke him out." He paced across the room and back, came to the desk, and, whirling the swivel chair, sank down into it. " 'A drop of ink may make a million think.' That's Byron."

Riley came to the desk. "Daniels, some of the boys are going to weaken like Buckner did and Clyde's doing. The cash money that the syndicate's offering is a hell of a temptation, but beef's bound to come back and they'll be sorry they let go. That's where you come in."

"I'll write it pretty." Daniels waggled a long forefinger at Riley. "Now let me tell you something. You're not as popular as you would have been if you'd come back with the money. You didn't help your position by standing up for Sand. You'll be in hell whichever way you jump, but if you go back on your conscience, you'll be in the deepest hell there is."

Daniels rose and, taking the whiskey bottle from his pocket, set it on the shelf. "Courage builder," he said scornfully. "All it ever did was to give me something to hide behind." He turned his gaze to Riley. "Your example is the only real courage builder there is in these parts. You stick to what you believe in, and I'll see that every man on the Flat keeps watching you."

Embarrassed, Riley said: "Better toss that bottle through the window."

Daniels shook his head. "No. I'll keep it there to show that I'm bigger than it is." He walked around the stove and swung back to face Riley again. "I know how deep into hell a man can go. I've been there. I've got to lick that bottle and I've got to lick something else."

Riley watched him stride on back to the press, come around the paper cutter, and return to the front of the room. A strange man, Riley thought, and a talented one, but in spite of his fine words, Riley doubted if he would stick for a week.

Daniels dropped into the swivel chair again. "There's something about Wheeler's murder that seems queer. It was quiet just then. Nobody on the street but you and Sand. Wheeler ran out and called to you. You called back and started toward him. That right?"

Riley nodded. "Go on."

"Neither you nor Sand was looking up. There wasn't anybody in position to see the shot, but it sounded as if it came from above me."

"Hey, Riley." It was the hotel clerk standing in the doorway.

Riley turned. "Oh, hello, Jake."

The clerk held out a folded sheet of paper. "For you."

Riley took it, muttered—"Thanks, Jake,"—still thinking of what Daniels had said. "Somebody could have been on the hotel roof."

36

"And somebody could have been in one of the front rooms of the hotel," Daniels added.

Riley unfolded the note.

I want to see you, Dan. Don't you want to see me?

Tana

Riley raised his eyes to Daniels as he slipped the paper into his pocket, that strange feeling of being in the middle of a nightmare creeping into him. All the hotel rooms above the street were rented by Tana Marlowe.

Tana Marlowe was a strange and mysterious woman for a cow town like Harmony. He was, Riley thought, the only person on the Flat who knew her. She had lived in the hotel for six months, she seldom left her rooms except to take a ride, and her meals were brought up to her. Now, crossing the hotel lobby and climbing the stairs, Riley told himself that he didn't really know her, either. It was beyond his understanding why a beautiful woman like Tana would exile herself in her rooms the way she had done.

Riley knocked on the door of Tana's living room. When she called out for him to come in, he opened the door, stepped in, closed it behind him.

Tana was standing by the windows, a tall,

graceful woman with hair as black as midnight, her dark eyes shining.

For a moment they stood motionless, each looking at the other. Riley laboring for breath. It was always that way when he saw her. She was like a drink of strong wine to him. That, too, was something he didn't understand, for no other woman had ever affected him that way.

She came to him with her graceful flowing way of walking, red lips softly pressed. She said in a caressing voice: "Dan, it's been so long."

He took her in his arms and kissed her, her long body molded against his, her arms around him, and she swept Dan Riley into another world where he could forget his failure and his troubles. Then she drew her lips from his and looked at him, a soft palm coming up to touch his cheek.

She said again: "Dan, it's been so long." She took his hand and led him to an orange love seat. This was her furniture, walnut and rosewood with plush velvet coverings on the love seat and chairs.

"What luck did you have, Dan?"

"No luck," Riley said.

She sighed and relaxed against him. "I knew you wouldn't have. I could have told you before you started, but they had to find out, didn't they?"

"How did you know?"

She rose and walked across the room to the rosewood table. She stood there for a moment, fingering a red hollyhock blossom. There were few flowers in Harmony, but when any could be found, she insisted that they be sent to her.

"I know a great deal about business, Dan," Tana said at last. "We like to think we have laws that protect the weak, but actually our laws are shaped to protect those who have money so they can make more money. That's the way it is when we suffer what they call a panic. The rich can buy when prices are low. The poor man is squeezed out. I know the rules of the game, Dan. That's the way I aim to play it."

He stared at her, puzzled. "You aim to play what?" he asked.

She smiled. "Business, Dan."

He rose and walked toward her. "I didn't come up here to talk business."

He reached for her, but she turned and walked around the table. "Listen, Dan. It's been nice . . . all the kissing and the loving . . . so nice that it's time to get married."

He stopped, puzzled, and staring at her.

"Well, are you going to keep on staring at me as if I was a stranger?" Tana demanded with some sharpness. "Do I have to propose?"

"I told you I failed," he said, suddenly angry. "I can't propose to anyone." He made a sweeping motion. "Especially to a woman who's used to this kind of living."

"Oh, Dan, don't be a fool. You say you've

failed. All right. That means the little rancher is finished on the Flat. The syndicate will own it all before spring. I need you and you need me. It's as simple as that."

He couldn't take his eyes from her. He was seeing her as he had never seen her before—alluring but self-willed and scheming. "I guess you don't need me," he said.

"Of course I do, Dan. I didn't ask to be born a woman. I looked at myself and saw that I was, but I promised myself it wouldn't stop me. Still, there are some things even a woman can't do. Those are the things you can do for me."

He shook his head, and reached for tobacco and paper. "I guess I never knew you, Tana," he said reluctantly.

She laughed softly. "You know what I can give you, Dan, and I know what you can do for me. It's a fair bargain. Didn't you know I am the syndicate? All of it."

He was lifting the cigarette to his lips when she said that. He stood stock-still, a long breath sawing out of him, right hand holding the cigarette a foot from his mouth. "No, I didn't," he said in a low tone.

"Not many people around here do. Black Mike Sand does. Didn't you wonder why he obligingly sent the Skull hands out of town?"

He remembered Sand looking up at the hotel windows. "You gave him a signal?"

"Of course. I knew what you were asking him, and I don't want trouble at a time when you would be hurt. I want the Flat. I have the money to buy it, Dan. I'll pay a fair price. The best thing you can do for your neighbors is to persuade them to sell out."

He threw the cigarette across the room. "You don't need the Flat. Let us alone."

"I need it and I'll have it," she flung at him. "It will give us hay land we don't have now. It will give us access to summer range in the Blue Mountains. It means the difference between the ten thousand head of cattle we have now and the forty thousand I aim to own."

"You'll never get the Flat." Riley started toward the door.

She moved in front of him, cat-like in her quickness, and raised her hands to his shoulders. "When are we getting married, Dan? I'll do the proposing if I have to."

No, he had never really known her before. He had long noticed the feline grace with which she moved. Now he sensed a cruelty about her that was as feline as her slim body. It was not love in her black eyes. It was something else he did not want to name.

"Let's say it was a mistake, Tana."

"I always get what I want, Dan. You're part of it. You'll help me get the rest, and I'll make you the biggest man in Oregon. Isn't that fair?"

41

He had never been able to think straight when she was as close to him as now. A giddiness washed through him. She was, the way she saw it, offering him everything a man could want, everything except the right to keep his pride and the right to obey his conscience.

He pushed her away. He had to think straight now. "No. I made another bargain first."

"A bargain with your neighbors?" she jeered.

"That's right. We'll stick together."

She laughed. It was not a pleasant sound. "You *are* a simple, trusting fool, Dan. They won't stick any more than Bill Buckner did. Or Larry Clyde. Or George Farr in the Mercantile."

He took her hands away from his shoulders. "What about Farr?"

"He's done giving you credit."

"I don't believe you."

"Go ask him. I told you I knew the rules. Men made them, Dan, but I can play their way."

"Daniels said the shot that killed Ben Wheeler was fired from one of your rooms."

He saw her lips tighten, her dark eyes narrow, as she considered her answer before she made it. "I was in the lobby," she said at last, "writing that note for you when the shot was fired. The clerk will tell you that." She backed against the door, her cheeks fired with color as anger swept through her. "You're intimating I killed him?"

"No." He shook his head. "But I've heard a lot just now I didn't know. It might have been Hogan."

"It wasn't. Who's this Daniels you mentioned?"

"Andrew Daniels. He rode in on the stage with me. He's taking over the *Clarion*."

She was silent for a moment, as if shaken by the news.

"No!" she cried. "He'll ruin me, Dan. Send him out of town."

"You can talk to Daniels yourself," Riley said bitterly. "Maybe you'll kiss him and make another slave out of him like you have the rest."

"Don't say that, Dan."

He took an arm and started to pull her away from the door. "I've got a job to do," he told her harshly.

"What about us, Dan?" She fell against him, her lips seeking his. He kissed her fiercely, almost brutally. Then he picked her up and carried her to the love seat and dropped her.

"That was good bye," he announced.

Then he swung around and strode to the door. He had his hand on the knob when she said: "Dan!" It was a sharp word thrown at him.

"I told you it was good bye," he said.

"All right." She made a sweeping gesture as if she would wipe everything away that had gone between them. "Go home and look at yourself in the mirror, Dan. You'll see a fool who threw away the things that any other man would give half his life for."

"I'm not any other man, Tana," he said. "I'm Dan Riley."

"All right," she said again. "But just remember this. When I came here, Black Mike told me you were the key man on the Flat. So I stopped at your place for a drink. I invited you to my rooms. I made you make love to me. You know why? Because you were the key man and I needed you. Now there'll be another man to take what you're throwing in my face."

"Who?"

"Larry Clyde, and you can depend on something else. I'll never pull Mike Sand's men off again to save your life."

He went out, shutting the door behind him, and walked slowly along the hall and down the stairs, a dull throbbing sickness in him. Now he knew what had happened to Larry Clyde.

George Farr had been one of the first on the Flat along with Riley's father and John Blair. His mercantile had been the only store between Denio and Cañon City, and it had grown as the Flat was settled.

Farr came out of the back of the store when he heard Riley come in. He was a small, bald man whose wife had died the year before, and her death had left him cranky and discontented.

"That's a bad thing about Ben," Farr said. "Two shootings in less than a month."

"A hell of a bad thing, George. You see how it is, don't you? The syndicate is done playing."

"I guess the boys'll be selling and moving off the Flat." Farr's watery eyes were unable to meet Riley's. "You, too, I reckon."

"No." Riley looked along the shelves. There were more cans than he had expected to see. "How are you fixed on spuds? Sugar? Flour?"

The watery eyes were pinned on bolts of cloth across the room. "Not too good, but enough for them that's got cash."

"So it's true. I didn't believe it, George."

"Believe what?"

"That you were cutting credit off."

Farr tried to look at Riley then. "What can I do? All of you owe me. You had enough money to take a wild-goose chase to Portland and around to hell-an'-gone, but you don't have money to pay me. The syndicate's giving you a chance to get out with some *dinero* in your pockets." He paused and cleared his throat, then added: "Enough to pay your store bill."

"We've all got cattle, George. We've all got good ranches. Prices of beef will come back. You won't lose anything."

Farr shook his head. "I can't take the chance, Dan. I've worked a long time to make this

45

business. I ain't gonna gamble it away on the price of beef."

Riley stared across the counter at the little man, hating him and hating Tana Marlowe and the way she had with men.

"She's beautiful, ain't she, George?"

Farr jumped. The watery eyes widened as surprise shocked him. "Yes, she is," he answered after a few moments.

"She talked about marrying you, didn't she? You kissed her, and you thought you were a young man again, didn't you?"

Farr's fists clenched and opened. His lips trembled. He whispered: "You'd better drift, Dan."

"Sure, George," Riley breathed. "You watch how this thing comes out. If we win, you're the one who had better drift."

Riley swung out of the store and slanted across the street to the livery where he had stabled his horse. Blair and the others had left town. Funny, he thought as he stepped into the saddle, how many things can change in a month. He rode out of town, dull aching emptiness in him.

Riley reined into Rush Wilkes's yard. Wilkes was the sheriff, a fat old man who had always been a good sheriff because there had been few laws broken in the county since he had taken the star. He was sitting in a rocker under a cottonwood when Riley pulled up, the squeak of the chair a discordant spine-jarring sound.

Wilkes raised a pudgy hand in greeting. "Howdy, Dan. Heard you was back."

"Maybe you heard Ben was shot?"

"Yeah." Wilkes's eyes, almost hidden in their deep sockets, blinked uncertainly. "Too bad."

"Gonna look into it?"

"Thought I would," Wilkes said heavily. "I'm likewise thinking of getting me a deputy. Want the job?"

"No. If I took the star, it'd be the sheriff's. What do you know about Buckner's killing?"

"Not much. He'd just made a deal with Sand, and he had two thousand dollars in his pocket when he left the hotel. There's some time I can't account for after he left the hotel. Anyhow, he was shot in front of the Saddle Up, and his pockets were empty."

"He was killed in the street?"

Wilkes nodded. "Right smack out in the middle. He was in the patch of light from the saloon."

"Anybody see where the shot came from?"

Wilkes shifted in his rocker. "No. Nobody was outside."

"What was the bullet hole like?"

Again Wilkes shifted in his chair. He had been chewing on a match. He took it out of his mouth and snapped it in two between thick fingers. "Funny thing about that shot, Dan. The bullet ranged down like maybe it was shot from high up."

"Like maybe from a second-story hotel window?"

Wilkes lumbered to his feet. "That's just the notion I had, but them windows all belong to the Marlowe woman. If I said she shot him, you'd drill me."

"No, I wouldn't, Rush. I found out something today. The syndicate is Tana Marlowe."

Wilkes dropped back into his chair, hands on his knees, sweat a shiny film on his face. "That explains some things I've wondered about." He cleared his throat. "Thought you was sweet on her?"

Riley shook his head. "Any man can make a mistake. Larry Clyde's making one now."

"Yeah, I know. That sets hell up ready to pop, Dan. Stay away from Larry."

"I'm going to see him now. No use staying away from something, Rush. If I'm figuring it right, we ain't got much time."

Wilkes heaved himself out of his chair again. "I've been waiting for you to come back, Dan. I didn't go to town when I heard Ben was shot 'cause I figured you'd do all that could be done, but now I'm going to hitch up and drive into town. I want to ask Doc Medery about the slug that killed Ben Wheeler. Might be that slug slanted down just like the one that got Buckner."

"She didn't plug Ben. She was in the hotel lobby when it happened."

"A pretty face can make a lot of men do things they wouldn't do otherwise, Dan," Wilkes said impassively.

"Let me know if you need me, Rush," Riley said, and reined out of the yard.

Riley turned off the county road before he reached his DR, and followed a lane across a hay field to Clyde's Triangle C. He had no definite plan in mind, and he knew he would not be welcomed, but there had to be a showdown and the sooner it came the better.

Clyde was shoeing a horse. He must have seen Riley, for he came around the house and stood waiting under a cottonwood, a sour and angry man. He called: "Turn around and keep going, Dan. We've got nothing to talk about."

"Now maybe we have," Riley said, and kept on.

"You can't talk me out of selling!" Clyde bellowed. "Go on now. Vamoose."

"That's a hell of a way to talk to a friend," Riley said mildly. "We didn't get much chance to visit in town."

"I ain't aiming to visit with you now . . . and don't start talking about old times and loyalty and all that. I've played second fiddle to you long enough."

Then Riley had the answer. He had grown up with Larry Clyde, but Dan Riley had been the leader from the first, even back in their school days. Clyde had pretended to be his friend, but all the time jealousy had been a growing canker in him.

"Playing second fiddle ain't got nothing to do with us being friends, has it, Larry?" Riley stepped down and moved away from his horse so that he stood in the shade of the cottonwood. "I've kind of depended on you."

Clyde's right hand moved toward his gun butt. His red hair was a tousled mass on his head. His shirt front was stirred by his breathing. "You've been the big mucky-muck on this range for a long time, Dan," he said. "It's going to be different now."

"What's happened to you, Larry? I thought you were just the same when the stage got in."

A small smile touched Clyde's lips. "I was waiting to see if you had the money. You didn't, and that finished you and everything else on the Flat. From now on its Skull. I aim to keep on the winning side."

Irritation stirred Riley, but he held his voice even when he said: "She's right pretty, Larry, and when she kisses you, you feel big enough to lick the world for her."

Clyde stood motionless, surprise shocking him. "What are you talking about?"

"Tana, which same you knew. She rode in here one day and asked for a drink. She invited you to come see her. You did, and you've belonged to her ever since."

"You're jealous," Clyde flung at him. "You went after Tana because she was the prettiest woman on the Flat, but for once you didn't get what you went after. She'll marry me, Riley, and I'll be the biggest man in the county. That's why I mentioned her in town. I wanted Blair and all of 'em to know who she is. From now on you won't be playing both sides. You're with the Combine, and I'm with Tana."

"You crazy damned fool," Riley said. "Can't you see she's using you like she's using George Farr and like she's trying to use me?"

The last of Clyde's self-control went out of him. He grabbed for his gun, but he didn't get it out of leather. Riley hit him, knocking him back against the trunk of the cottonwood. He fell sideways, turned over, and tried for his gun again.

Riley jumped on him, one foot pinning his wrist to the ground.

"Behave, Larry," Riley said. "This ain't getting either one of us anything."

Riley stooped and picked up Clyde's gun. Clyde lay there, his eyes hating Riley, and he cursed him in a bitter, flaying voice. Riley stepped back, slipping the gun into his waistband. Clyde rolled over, came to his hands and knees, and lunged at

51

Riley, fists beating at him. Riley blocked a blow, took another on the chin, and, grabbing a handful of Clyde's shirt, shook him.

"Behave, Larry!" Riley shouted. "Damn it, you're acting like a kid."

Clyde's shirt was pulled out of his pants. He hit Riley again, and Riley, patience gone, struck him on the mouth and knocked him flat. That was when Riley saw the heavy money belt around Clyde's middle. He dropped on Clyde, knees driving wind from the other man, and stripped the belt from him.

"Where did you get this?" Riley demanded, an ugly suspicion in him. "Have you sold out to Skull?"

Clyde sat up, struggling for breath. Fear was in his green eyes, fear that was close to panic. He managed: "Not yet I ain't."

"How much is in here?"

"A thousand dollars. I got it playing poker."

"Don't lie, Larry. You're the worst poker player on the Flat."

Clyde came to his feet, his hand feeling his bruised face. "All right," he blurted. "I didn't get it playing poker, but it ain't none of your business how I did get it."

Riley threw the money belt on the ground at Clyde's feet. "I'm remembering some of the good times we've had together, Larry. I reckon that makes me the fool Tana said I was, but I'm

52

letting you go because that money ain't enough evidence to hang you." He walked back to his horse and stepped up. "You'd better get out of the country. Ben Wheeler was my friend."

Riley rode off, leaving Clyde staring after him and cursing in that dead tone.

Riley rode into his ranch yard, eyes searching the house, the log barn, the pole corrals. Only now did he realize how far things had gone. Bill Buckner had been robbed and murdered. Ben Wheeler had been murdered because his voice was dangerous to Skull, to the syndicate that was nothing more than a selfish, merciless woman. Now that Dan Riley had refused to be used by her, he had placed himself in a position from which he would have to be removed.

There seemed to be nothing wrong about the place. John Blair had promised to look after things while Riley was gone. Apparently he had. Riley's horses were in the pasture. His hay had been cut and stacked. No cattle were in sight, but that was the way it should be, for all the Combine stock had been driven into the Blue Mountains to the north.

Off-saddling, Riley led his mount into the corral and moved toward the house. That was when he saw the thin column of smoke rising from the chimney. He had not expected that. Anyone waiting in the house to dry-gulch him would not likely build a fire. Still, he could not be sure. Whoever was inside might think he would assume it was John Blair or one of his men.

The front door was closed. Riley drew his gun and, throwing the door open, lunged into the house. The room was empty. Warm air spiced by the smell of cooking food rushed at him. The floor had been recently scrubbed. The furniture had been dusted. The room had not looked like this since his mother died.

Noiselessly, Riley moved to the kitchen door and jerked it open. He smelled frying bacon, heard its sizzle, and then the gun sagged in his hand. He leaned against the door casing, breath sawing in and out of his lungs as relief washed through him. Connie Sand was bending over the stove.

She looked up, smiling, saw the gun and shook her head. "Do you always come into your house ready to shoot?"

Riley holstered his gun, lurched across the room, dropped into a chair. "Not usually. What are you doing here, Connie?"

She opened the oven door and popped a pan of biscuits inside. Then she straightened and raised a hand to her hair as if to feel whether it was in place.

"I wanted to make a friendly gesture, but I'll move on if you say to."

54

"Of course not. I just can't figure it out. How did Mike happen to let you do this?"

"I'm twenty-one, Dan." She turned the bacon in the frying pan. "The house was pretty dirty. Blair's man must have been a terrible housekeeper."

"Did John leave someone here?"

She nodded. "The man left when I came. I cleaned the front room up. I didn't have time to do any more." She pulled the coffee pot to the back of the stove. "I didn't think you'd eat in town with so much happening today. You didn't, did you?"

"No, but I don't . . ."

"All right. You don't understand." She faced him, frowning. "Dan, is there any reason we can't be friends? Or allies?"

"Plenty. Mike won't . . ."

"My father is a stubborn man, but murder is not his way. He had a fit when I told him about Hogan being at Ma O'Brien's this morning."

"Is Mike quitting Skull?"

"He'll have to. Or Skull will quit what's been going on behind Dad's back. Better wash up, Dan."

"I've got to get something straight first. I know that Tana Marlowe is the syndicate. What you're trying to say is that Mike won't stand for the antics she's been up to."

"That's it, Dan." She turned her back to him

55

and forked bacon into a plate. "Where do you stand?"

"I'm the one fellow on this range that nobody could mistake," he said with some heat. "How do you think I stand?"

"The talk is that you're in love with Tana. If that's true, you don't stand where folks think you do."

"I'm not in love with Tana. That was finished the minute she said she was the syndicate."

He heard her take a long breath.

"Wash up, Dan."

"Looks like we're sort of on the same side."

She looked at him, her face held very sober. "Sort of."

He saw that she was troubled. He went on through the back door to the porch and washed up. There was little talk until after they had eaten and Riley had caught her horse and saddled him for her.

"I'm not superstitious, Dan," she said as she prepared to leave, "and I don't believe in premonitions, but I know something is going to happen. It's got to. I guess that's the real reason I came here today. Dad wouldn't like it if he knew I was asking for help, but I think we'll need it."

"Looks to me like we're the ones needing help."

She shook her head. "Anybody who works for Tana Marlowe needs help. I've known about her for a long time. She made a lot of money in her gambling place in San Francisco, and this is her idea of how to be respectable. The trouble is she's using the same methods she's always used."

"Didn't Mike know what he'd be in for?"

"He says he didn't," she said somberly. "It was a good job, and she promised she'd leave everything in his hands. Well, she couldn't. She isn't built that way."

She stepped into the saddle, gave him a small smile, and rode away.

Riley found sleep elusive that night. Once, he got up and stood in the doorway, looking across the night-shrouded flat. There was a light in John Blair's house. That was all, and presently that winked out.

He went back to bed and lay staring into the blackness, trying to guess what Tana Marlowe would do. He thought of Larry Clyde, and he stopped trying to see ahead. There was no guessing what a man like Clyde would do, for Clyde had been hating him all the time that he had been pretending to be his friend.

Later he went to sleep and almost immediately was awake again, the pound of a galloping horse in his ears. He pulled on his pants and grabbed his gun. He heard Connie Sand's call as he headed for the door.

"Dan, Dan!" She was off her horse before he

was able to open the door. She stopped, stumbled and almost fell, before she could regain her footing.

He came out of the house, shouting: "Here, Connie!"

She ran toward him. She was out of breath, but her voice was tightly controlled. "They killed Dad tonight, Dan. They're going after that man who took Ben Wheeler's place. Tana got word to Clyde. She said she would pick the next editor."

She stood before him, holding back her tears, a small straight figure in the starlight.

He put his hands on her arms, saying: "Tell me about it."

"Clyde came over about dusk. Dad had sent all the men but Hogan to Whispering Springs to move some cattle. Clyde said you knew too much. Hogan said they'd get you and Daniels, and it would be over with. Dad said there would be no more killings and told Hogan he was fired. Hogan said he was taking orders straight from Tana. I didn't hear all of it then, but they quarreled and Hogan shot Dad. Then they left to get the men at Whispering Springs."

"You're sure your dad is dead?"

"He died in my arms," she said, still speaking quietly. "He told me Clyde admitted killing Buckner and Wheeler. Clyde and Hogan had fixed it so that Hogan robbed Buckner when he left the hotel. Clyde was upstairs in one of Tana's rooms waiting to shoot Buckner as soon as he got into the light. It was Clyde who shot at your friends and sent the warning notes."

Suddenly she let her breath out in a long sob and began to cry. He held her in his arms, wanting to comfort her, but thinking of the distance to Whispering Springs and back to town. He put his hand under her chin.

"Connie, can you ride over to Blair's place?"

"I . . . I could, Dan." The quiet control came back to her voice. "But I . . ."

"Are you willing to fight on the side of the little ranchers, or do you think we're all through?"

"I . . . I don't know what to think, Dan," she whispered. "Dad always said . . ."

"Will you go over to Blair's place? Tell him to round our men up. I've got to go to town."

She drew her head back, as if trying to see him. "I'll go, Dan," she breathed, "but he'll never believe me."

"You've got to make him believe you. There isn't much time."

It took Riley only a moment to stop at the sheriff's place and get him out of bed.

"I'll ride over to Blair's house and bring the men in," Wilkes promised. "Get Daniels out of town. We'll be ready for Hogan's bunch."

Riley went on to Harmony, cracking steel to his horse at every jump. Time was running out.

59

Getting Andrew Daniels out of town wasn't the answer. If Hogan burned the print shop, there would be no paper, and the story of this night's happenings must be told. Tana Marlowe had every reason to fear the *Clarion*'s power.

There were these few moments to think before he reached Harmony, and he didn't like the conclusion logic forced him to make. Black Mike Sand had been the one retarding influence on Tana Marlowe's lust for power and wealth. Now that he was gone, Hogan would take over and Hogan was a killer. Larry Clyde, jealous and drunk with his desire for Tana, would be worse.

Dawn was beginning to show in the east when Riley turned into the livery stable. He stepped down, asking the sleepy-eyed hostler if anyone had ridden into town lately. Hogan and Clyde must have expected to do more than kill Andrew Daniels or they wouldn't have gone after the Skull crew. On the other hand, they might have changed their minds and come directly to Harmony.

"Been plumb quiet, Dan," the hostler said. "Expecting trouble?"

"A lot of it," Riley answered, and, turning into the street, walked rapidly toward the *Clarion* office.

Riley's boot heels beat upon the walk with pistol-like sharpness. There was no other sound except the insistent crowing of a rooster to his right. He opened the front door of the *Clarion*'s office, saw Daniels's lanky body bent over the desk, a lighted lamp in front of him, and his first thought was that the man was drunk.

"Daniels!" Riley shouted.

Daniels raised his head, shook it, and grabbed for a .45 that lay before him.

Riley shouted: "Take it easy!"

"Oh, it's you." Daniels rose and rubbed his eyes. "Guess I dropped off."

The whiskey bottle on the shelf was still full. Riley asked: "What are you doing up?"

"I thought she would send her killers after me before now." Daniels ran his fingers over the top of his head. "I intended to be ready for them. What brings you here?"

Riley looked at him, puzzled. "What she?"

Daniels waved toward the hotel. "The woman you call Tana Marlowe. I knew her by another name in San Francisco. You might as well know, Riley. It was not accident that brought me here. I heard that she was in Harmony. It would be fitting and proper if I shot her, but I am not a woman-killer. Besides, it would be better if I destroyed her plans, and I can do that through the *Clarion*."

Riley remembered Tana saying Daniels would ruin her. He asked: "You mean you're not just a drunk looking for a job?"

"A drunk?" Daniels's smile held a strange

deep bitterness. "I guess I'm that. She has a face as beautiful as an angel and a heart as wicked as hell. She causes misery wherever she goes. I knew there would be misery here. I had a great future once. . . ." He shrugged and spread his hands in a weary futile gesture. "My story wouldn't interest you. I came here looking for the job I've got, and circumstances threw it into my lap. If her men don't kill me first, I'll see that she doesn't stay in Harmony."

"Have you seen her?" Riley asked.

Daniels nodded. "I went over to the hotel as soon as you left town. I told her what I meant to do. I think she didn't sleep well tonight." The smile touched his lips again, self-mocking. "You see, Riley, I was in love with her once. It was a great love on my part, and for a time she found in me what she wanted. That was only as long as my paper and my connections were useful to her."

Riley wheeled toward the door, saying over his shoulder: "They're on their way now. Keep that gun handy."

"Where are you going?"

Riley didn't answer. He ran toward the hotel. He wasn't sure there was time, but it was the only way he could play it. Tana Marlowe could save the town and the Combine.

Riley took the hotel stairs two at a time, swung down the hall, and knocked on the door of Tana's sitting room.

"Who is it?" came her voice.

"Dan Riley."

There was silence for a moment. He knew that doubts were in her, but he thought that in the end her belief in her own power over men would win. He was right. The lock clicked and she swung the door open.

"So you've come back to me, Dan."

She stood in the doorway, a tall, straight figure, her black hair down her back. She was wearing a dark, tight-fitting robe and Riley thought of what Daniels had said about her not sleeping well tonight.

"I came back, but not to you," he said harshly. "You're coming with me."

"What do you want, Dan?"

"We're going to the *Clarion* office."

Breath burst out of her in a sigh. "Oh, no, Dan! I don't know what Daniels has told you, but it's all a lie."

"Come on."

He reached for her hand. She leaped back, pulling a small gun from her pocket. He caught her wrist and twisted until the gun clattered on the floor. She slapped at him with her left hand. He kept his grip on her right wrist, tried to grab her left, but she clawed at him, fingernails leaving bloody scratches on the side of his face. He had her then, both arms pinned, and carried her out of the room.

"Let me down!" she screamed, while kicking and trying to break free.

He got one hand over her mouth, and, in spite of her kicking and twisting, carried her down the stairs.

The clerk jumped up, shouting: "What the hell, Riley . . . !"

"Stay out of it," Riley said coldly, and went into the street. The sound of many horses came to him from the south.

Suddenly she relaxed, and became soft and pliant in his arms. She whispered: "You did come back to me, Dan. We'll go away together. Anywhere. I told you I didn't ask to be born a woman, but I was, and it's foolish to act as if I was anything else. We belong to each other, Dan."

He carried her into the *Clarion* office and put her on her feet. He kicked the door shut. "Tana, Black Mike Sand was shot and killed," he said. "Hogan and Clyde are on their way here with your crew. What are you going to do?"

"I don't believe Black Mike was shot," she cried. "He's the kind who's indestructible."

"Connie told me. You had to have him for one purpose and you needed Hogan for another, but you couldn't work them together. Now you're finished."

She smiled. "No, Dan. I'm not finished. I always win, don't I, Andy?"

Daniels stood back of the desk, a tall, silent man. Only his eyes, fixed on the woman, seemed alive.

"Tell him, Andy," she said.

"Yes, I'll tell him." Still he looked at her, the agony of all his memories in his eyes. "I'll tell everybody. I have it set up. It took me most of the night."

Wheeling, Daniels picked up a sheet of copy paper and rolled it across the type he had set. Peeling it off, he turned back to her. "You always wanted one thing you never got," he said hoarsely. "Respectability. You used to think I could give it to you, but I couldn't. Then you were done with me. You sold out and came up here. You thought it would be a new country where you could buy the power you wanted, but you couldn't lick yourself. You went at it in the same old way." He held up the sheet of copy. "I've told it here. They'll all know it when the next issue of the *Clarion* goes to press."

She put a hand out to him. "Don't hound me, Andy. Give me a chance."

The horses were close now. Riley said: "You've got your chance. Call off your wolves."

She whirled to face him. "I will, Dan. Make Daniels destroy what he wrote."

"Don't believe her, Riley!" Daniels shouted. "Don't believe anything she ever promises. She's got to be destroyed."

But Riley wasn't sure. "She's our only chance, Daniels. Blow out the lamp."

Daniels hesitated. There was silence, the three of them standing motionless, silence except for the hammer of horses' hoofs. Daniels lunged toward the desk then and blew out the lamp before saying: "You can't trust her, Riley. I tell you . . . you can't trust her."

Tana's soft hand was on Riley's arm. "He hates me, Dan. You can trust me. I'll show you."

Riley drew his gun and threw the door open. "We'll see."

They were in the street now, a packed mass of horses, Hogan and Clyde in front. The sun had tipped up over the eastern hills, throwing a red glint upon the street.

Riley called: "Hold up, Hogan."

With his call Hogan and Clyde drew guns, Hogan shouting: "This is luck, Larry! We'll get 'em both."

As long as Dan Riley lived, he would never know for sure what was in Tana Marlowe's mind. She ran past him into the street.

"Don't, Hogan," she cried out.

That was the way Tana Marlowe died. Hogan and Clyde had guns in their hands, hammers back. They caught the blur of motion and fired before they saw who it was. Tana screamed and fell.

Riley was in the doorway, his gun roaring,

tongues of flame leaping from the muzzle. His first shot knocked Flint Hogan out of his saddle and under the feet of the horses behind him. Daniels broke glass from a window and his shot got Larry Clyde. Leaderless, the rest of the Skull crew began firing, but without order or system. Riley did not waste a bullet. Every shot emptied a saddle. Lead chipped the door casing beside his head. Other slugs whined past him. One tugged at his shoulder. Another seared his side with white heat. Daniels cried out and fell, then lifted himself again and kept shooting.

There was this one moment of chaos, of screaming lead and flashes of flame and the thunder of guns. Then other guns from the end of the street, and the Combine roared into town. Skull broke under the double pressure and fled past the *Clarion* office, seeking escape in the open country beyond the town.

Riley's Colt was empty. He watched them go, a wolf pack that had lost its bite. The Combine flashed past, the sheriff in front, John Blair beside him, hatless, white hair and beard caught by the wind. Then they were gone, and the sound of the guns faded.

Riley moved into the street, picked Tana up, and brought her inside. She still had strength to lift an arm and lay her hand against his cheek.

"I can die now, Dan," she whispered. "I tried to

do one decent thing." Then she went slack in his arms.

Daniels, bleeding from a chest wound, crawled to Riley.

"She's gone?" he murmured.

"Gone," Riley confirmed, and, carrying her into the back room, laid her on the bed. When he returned, Daniels had pulled himself to his feet. He had torn up the copy that told Tana's story.

"I'll do that over, Riley," he said. "I won't hound her anymore. I'll write her story again, and I'll make it pretty."

Doc Medery and other townsmen were in the room, filled with questions that Riley did not feel like answering. He was quiet as the medico worked on him. But he could not keep his thoughts from Tana Marlowe. He asked himself why she had run into the street. It might have been to stop Flint Hogan and his men. That was the way Dan Riley liked to think of it.

"What happened?" they asked.

"It's finished," was all Riley could say, and when his wounds had been dressed, he walked slowly down the boardwalk to the stable. When he rode into the street, Blair and the others were back, and George Farr stood in front of the Mercantile.

"Is she dead?" Farr asked.

Riley nodded.

"I'm drifting," Farr said in a dry whisper, his face wiped clean of expression. He threw a key at Riley. "Help yourself." Wheeling blindly, he lurched down the street.

"Where's Connie?" Riley asked.

"Waiting for you at your place," Blair said. "Dan, I guess that ends it."

"We still don't have money and the price of beef ain't up any," Riley said, "but when my folks were alive, we had a way of working together and money didn't count for much."

"We'll make out, and we'll see Farr gets paid for what we eat," Blair said.

Riley rode out of town then.

When he reached his ranch yard, Connie was waiting for him.

"Breakfast is ready," she told him.

He stepped down and walked toward her. "About the day of the small cowman being gone," he said. "Well, we've all got small outfits, but we used to make a pretty good living on the Flat. I've got a hunch we still can when beef prices come back. I keep hoping you could change your mind."

"Why, Dan, I can think the way my menfolk do. I've never been a managing woman."

She came to him and lifted her lips to his, and the morning sunlight, filled with promise, was bright upon them.

Valley of the 99

I

To cherish an ambition when it is a vague dream is one thing; to struggle with it in terms of sweat and tired muscles in the shadow of failure is another. As Rod Devers dug out the spring that had been mudded up the night before and repaired the pole enclosure which surrounded it, he wondered moodily if he had been smart or just plain stupid in starting his Rocking R here along the northern edge of Egan Valley. But smart or not, he knew that if he hadn't settled here, he would have tried it somewhere else.

As long as he could remember, Rod had been obsessed by the ambition to own a spread. That was why he had hired his gun and bargained with death for the highest wages he could get, saving his money until he had enough to buy a small herd. He had been twenty-four when he had come to the valley three years ago, content to hang up his gun. He'd found what he wanted—a flowing spring and pines and a hay meadow below the cabin site—so exactly what he wanted that he had the weird feeling that some unseen power had guided him here.

The day was hot even for late June, and sweat made a constant drip down Rod's face as he worked. By the time he finished, the sun was low in the west and shadows had crawled across the clearing until they reached the spring. He tossed his hammer into the grass, sourly considering the fact that this was the fourth time the spring had been mudded up. There had been other things, too, little pestering things that got under a man's hide.

The knowledge that he would have been all right if he had been content to wait didn't sweeten his temper. He hadn't been getting ahead fast enough, not fast enough to marry Doll Nance anyhow, and that was why he'd got his tail in a crack. If a man had enough pride to be worth a damn, he wouldn't marry a woman until he could support her. But Doll was a little short on patience.

Early in the spring Rod had borrowed two thousand dollars from Jason Abbot, the Poplar City horse trader, giving his herd as security. He'd used the money to buy a herd of two-year-old heifers in Warner Valley. Right now two thousand dollars looked like a million.

The note was due the 1st of September, and although Abbot had promised Rod more time if he needed it, the man might not keep his word. Beef prices had dropped, and what they would be in the fall was anybody's guess. It was that uncertainty which had planted the suspicion in Rod's mind that Abbot was responsible for these "accidents," hoping to discourage Rod so he'd sell his original herd and the heifers for about fifty cents on the dollar and get out with what he could.

Rod was not aware that his neighbor, Sam Kane, had ridden out of the pines above the spring until the man called: "Howdy, Rod!"

Startled, Rod turned. "Howdy, Sam," he said, and waited while Kane rode down the slope.

Reining up, Kane nodded at the broken poles on the ground that Rod had replaced. He said: "Looks like it happened again."

"Some damned horse leaned too hard," Rod said.

Kane swung down, his red, square face grim. "Got any notion who's doing it?"

Kane might have done it himself, for he was one of Abbot's best friends—or Todd Shannon, who lived west of Rod's Rocking R and would do anything for a quick dollar. It might even be Abbot and the two boys who rode for him. But these were all guesses, based on nothing more than Rod's vague uneasiness about the money he owed Abbot.

Rod shook his head. "No notion at all."

Kane leaned on the top pole, staring at the water that was forming a new channel in the mud below the spring. He was a chunky man twenty years older than Rod, hard-working, bull-headed, and given to forcing his opinion on his neighbors.

His SK lay a couple of miles to the east. Rod had ridden with him on roundup; they had swapped work at haying time. But Rod had promised himself they'd never do it again. To Sam Kane there were only two ways of doing anything, his way and the wrong way.

"Your trouble's just starting," Kane said ominously. "You heard about Karl Hermann coming?"

"I ain't heard nothing else since we knew he was looking over his layouts on the Malheur."

"You're a mite proddy," Kane murmured. "Anything else happen to sour your temper?"

"The fence between me and Todd Shannon's place was down again last night and his cows got into my hay field. A little more of that and I won't be cutting no hay this year."

Kane straightened, putting his back to the poles, and pulled a briar pipe out of his pocket. "Want to know who's doing it?"

"You bet I want to know."

Kane filled his pipe and slipped the tobacco can into his pocket. "Chances are you'll get sore."

"I'll listen."

"How well do you know your brother George?"

"If you think George . . ."

"Yeah, I figured you'd take it that way," Kane said.

"Me and George get along pretty well," Rod said, "providing there's a few miles between us, which there usually is. But there's one thing about George . . . he ain't sneaky."

"You should know," Kane shrugged. "The point is that trouble don't always start big. You see a little cloud in the sky and pretty soon you've got a hell of a storm on your hands. Well, I rode over to see where you stand."

"You ought to know without me telling you," Rod snapped.

Kane shook his head. "Not with your brother rodding Spade for Karl Hermann. Worth a hundred million dollars, Hermann is, but he ain't satisfied. Once he gets a toehold on a range, he keeps working on it till he's got it all."

"You've been listening to Jason Abbot."

"You'd best do some listening, too." Kane lighted his pipe and pulled hard on it for a moment. "You and me and Otto Larkin and the rest of us are nesters to a man like Hermann. We're just squatting, so Hermann will claim that the whole damned valley north of Spade is open range."

Impatient with the man's fears, Rod said: "You don't know what he'll claim."

Kane took the pipe out of his mouth, a bitter, worried man. "If you wasn't important, Rod, I wouldn't have bothered riding over here. There's some like your friend Frank Benson who ain't worth a damn. They'll move on, but I figured you're one who'll stick."

Rod stared at Kane's grim face, not sure what the man was actually driving at. Frank Benson was Rod's best friend, his spread lying between Rod's Rocking R and Kane's SK. Frank was the kind who would go hunting or get drunk the day they started roundup, and a little of that went a long way with Sam Kane, whose only standard of measurement was the amount of work a man did.

"You trying to make me sore . . . dragging Frank into this?" Rod asked.

Kane shook his head. "I'm just talking plain. You're cranky as hell today, but there's one more thing I'm gonna say. You're a good man to have on our side if it comes to a fight."

"Damn it, we ain't got a fight yet. Not with Hermann."

"We will . . . soon as he gets here. I'm just trying to lay this out the way I see it. It's the little fellows like you and me who'll stick it out through the bad years, the ones that'll make a country amount to something. We'll fight for what's ours, and to hell with Karl Hermann."

You're overlooking one thing," Rod said. "I ain't found out who I'm fighting."

"It's Hermann and your brother George, I tell you!" Kane shouted. "We all know you've been a gunfighter. We want you on our side and they want you out of the country so you won't be on

78

our side. That's the reason they keep pestering you. They figure you'll light out of the valley."

Kane had let his pipe go cold in his hand. He was watching Rod's lean face closely as if trying to read his mind.

Rod picked up his shovel and hammer, the thought striking him that Jason Abbot might have sent Kane here with this cock-and-bull yarn about George.

"All right," Rod said. "Go tell Abbot you spoke your piece."

"He's got nothing to do with me being here," Kane said sullenly. "It's time somebody was taking a lead, so I'm doing it. We're having a meeting in the Palace tonight to organize. When Hermann gets here, we'll tell him we're working together and we'll swap slug for slug. I want you to be at that meeting."

"No," Rod said. "I don't want any part of it."

"Then you're against us." Kane knocked his pipe out and put it into his pocket. "Looks like Hermann sent you here in the first place."

Rod fought his temper for a moment, wanting to kick Kane off the ranch, a desire which was balanced by the knowledge that it wouldn't do any good. Probably it was the very thing Abbot wanted, to separate Rod from his neighbors so that he stood alone.

"You're talking like a kid," Rod said, and turned away.

"Wait." Kane grabbed his arm. "I reckon I am at that."

Rod jerked free, wondering about this. He had never known Kane to come so close to admitting he was wrong about anything.

"Sam," he said, "when Karl Hermann steps on my toes, I'll fight. Not before."

"Look at it my way," Kane said. "You're young enough to start over. But I'm not, and I've got a wife to think about. If I lose out here, I'll never get another chance."

Kane was an obstinate man with the mental capacity for only one idea at a time. Rod hadn't thought the man was afraid of anything, but he saw that Kane was afraid now, and he began to understand. Most of the nesters had tried somewhere else and failed. Sam Kane was haunted by the fear that Karl Hermann would somehow make him fail again.

"Call off your meeting, Sam," Rod said. "Let's wait till Hermann gets here and see what he does."

"I reckon you're blind because it's your brother who's rodding Spade for Hermann," Kane said bleakly. "Well, I've got just one more thing to say. I've never killed a man in my life, but I'll kill one man or a dozen to hold what little I've got. Egan Valley is about the last place where a man can bring a few head of cows and make a start. Nobody's gonna drive me out."

"Nobody's trying."

"Jason says . . ." Kane stopped, scowling as if he regretted naming Abbot. "We're on the same side, Rod. Don't go over to Hermann."

"Did the notion ever strike you that Abbot's got a game of his own up his sleeve?"

Sullen now, Kane said: "Leave Jason out of this."

"I'm willing to, if he'll stay out. Tell him that. And tell him that if I ever prove what I suspicion about him, I'll put a window in his ornery, sneaking skull."

Rod walked away, and this time Kane let him go. When Rod reached the timber below the spring, he looked around and saw that Kane was riding back the way he had come. For a moment Rod watched him, his square body hunched forward dejectedly in the saddle.

A keen sense of regret touched Rod. Kane had a following in the valley. Trouble would come regardless of Hermann's intentions, for when a man like Kane was haunted by the fear of persecution as he was, he would not be satisfied until he had the trouble he expected.

Rod followed the small stream that was flowing again, the close-growing pines making a covering overhead and shadowing the trail so that it was nearly dark. The ground sloped sharply here, and when he came out of the pines above his cabin, he saw the shine of lamplight in the back window. Frank Benson had come over and was getting supper, Rod thought.

The sun was down now, twilight laying its purple hue upon the valley that stretched for miles below him, the opposite rim blotted from sight by the haze of distance. Spade's buildings lay twenty miles from here, close to the south shore of Egan Lake and not far from the sand reef which formed the west side of the lake. If that reef ever went out, thousands of acres of lake bottom would be exposed. It might never happen, but if it did, Karl Hermann would have trouble. Kane and his neighbors had talked about it, knowing it would be the best hay land in the valley. They would move onto it, claiming Spade had no right to it, but Hermann was not likely to see it that way.

Hermann had bought Spade from old Clay Cummings, who had got himself so deeply in debt by picking too many losers on California racetracks that he had been lucky to get anything for his spread.

At this moment George Devers would be having supper in the big ranch house, a good supper served by his Chinese cook.

Anger rose in Rod as it invariably did when he thought about his brother, who always picked the easy way. He wanted to be comfortable, have good wages, give orders to the *vaqueros* who rode for Spade. He hadn't a worry in the world. Well, it was a good life for George, but it wouldn't do for Rod.

He stepped into the shed behind his cabin and leaned the shovel against the wall. He slammed the hammer down on the work bench, making a loud clatter. He went out, realizing he wasn't being altogether fair to George, who only wanted one thing from life while he wanted another, for George possessed little of the independent spirit which characterized Rod.

Actually the resentment Rod felt toward George was not due to his choosing security instead of independence, for that was a man's privilege. The trouble went back to the time when their father had lost his Nevada ranch to one of Karl Hermann's banks and had died a few months later, frustrated and disappointed.

George had gone to work for Hermann, saying frankly that if you couldn't lick a man, you might just as well throw in with him. That, to Rod, was unforgivable. He'd told George what he thought of him and left the country. After that they had seen each other only occasionally, and then usually by accident.

After Rod had settled here in Egan Valley, George had paid him an unexpected visit. He had stayed only a day or two, their talk casual and impersonal, and when he had left, he had ridden south across Spade, which at the time had belonged to Clay Cummings. Within a month Hermann had bought Spade and sent George north to run it. That had been two years ago, and during those two years, Rod had not seen George except on a few Saturday afternoons when they had met on Poplar City's Main Street and exchanged greetings.

Rod came around the corner of the cabin, trying to forget George and telling himself he was glad Frank had come over. Then he saw that two horses were racked in front, and he quickened his steps, wondering. The door was open, lamplight making a yellow stain on the bare earth of the yard. He caught the smell of frying ham, and heard the sound of a girl's bright laughter.

Blood began to pound in his temples. Doll Nance was here!

In the doorway, Rod stopped and put a bony shoulder against the jamb. The table was set for three. Frank Benson and the girl stood by the stove, their backs to him, neither aware that he was there. He stood motionless for a moment, the poignant pleasure that just looking at her gave him beginning to die. He was afraid to ask why she had come.

Doll was twenty, a small girl whose head came only to Frank's shoulder. Rod had started going with her within a month after he had come to the valley. They had been engaged for a year, and now it seemed to Rod that he had never known or cared for any other girl. She was straightforward and direct and he had liked that, but she was impetuous and strong-willed, too, and that bothered him. Her sense of humor was as crazy and unpredictable as Frank's, and there were times when he couldn't tell when she was serious or when she was raw-hiding him.

Their last date had been a stormy one, for she could not see any connection between their marriage and the fact that Rod owed Jason Abbot two thousand dollars. She had said some biting things about his overgrown pride, and, after thinking about them for a week, he was still uncertain whether she had meant them or not.

He spoke her name.

She whirled, surprised and frightened because she had not known he was there. Then she laughed.

"Why did you sneak up like a Paiute? Who'd you think you'd find?"

"I didn't know. I have a different girl waiting for me every night."

Frank grinned down at Doll. "Don't get jealous. He lies common and regular, just like he breathes."

Doll grabbed up a butcher knife and flourished it. "If I ever find another woman with you, I'll scalp her from top to toe." She put the knife down. "Watch the ham, Frank," she said, and, crossing the room to Rod, lifted her mouth to be kissed. "Pay attention to your business, Mister Devers."

He did, and when she drew her lips away from his, he asked: "Satisfactory?"

"Very satisfactory, Mister Devers." She put a hand up to his mouth and he kissed the tip of each finger. "I came to tell you that I'm available for marriage tomorrow at high noon."

So that was why she had come. Looking down at her, he sensed the tension that had crept into her.

He said lightly: "I'll put it in my date book. I'd better wash up. Looks like supper's about ready."

He walked past her to the bench at the end of the stove, poured water into the wash pan, and scrubbed his face. When he dried and turned toward the table, he saw that Doll was forking ham from the frying pan onto a platter. He sat down, bone weary. The irritation that this day had brought to him began to give way to a sense of well-being. It was good to have supper ready when he got in. He could have it this way every night if he hadn't got himself into debt up to his neck, but there was no use thinking about that now.

He sat slack in his chair, watching Frank pour the coffee and return to the stove with the pot, walking in his awkward, lumbering way. Maybe Frank was lazy and careless, but he wasn't a sneak like Todd Shannon and he wasn't a bullhead like Sam Kane. Big and easy-going, he was pleasant company, and Rod had often been thankful they were neighbors.

Doll took biscuits from the oven and glanced over her shoulder to smile at Rod. She said: "I swiped one of Ma's pies. It'll be good, even if my cooking isn't."

"What kind?"

"Dried apple." Doll winked at Frank. "I've got him interested. Now I'm going to walk right through his stomach to his heart. I hear that's the way it's done."

"Even if it takes your ma's pies to do it," Rod said.

Doll brought the ham and biscuits to the table and stopped, hands on her hips, a hint of a smile lingering at the corners of her mouth as she looked at him. She wasn't pretty, Rod thought. Her lips were full and red, but too long. Her freckled nose was on the pug side. Her auburn hair was loosely pinned at the back of her head, and now, standing close to the lamp, the light made a bright shine on the film of sweat that covered her forehead.

"Let's get along with each other, Rod," she said. "For tonight?"

She said it as if it were a question, and he sensed that she wasn't quite certain of herself, but that she was resolved not to quarrel about their wedding date—for the moment at least.

He said: "Why sure, we'll get along." Then he winked at her.

"Nothing but peace and quiet." Frank laughed. "You had me worried, Rod. Thought you was mad at something."

Frank liked to laugh whether there was anything funny or not, and suddenly Rod wished he was anywhere but here. "I'm not mad," Rod said. "The spring was mudded up again and one side of the fence was busted all to hell."

"Any tracks?" Frank asked.

"A horse done it, which don't prove nothing. Then Sam Kane rides over and wants to fight Karl Hermann before Hermann even gets here."

Doll brought a dish of beans to the table. "What are you going to do?"

"Nothing, till I get my hands on the gent who's been making my accidents."

"My tapeworm sure is a-hollering." Frank sat down at the table. "How long have I got to keep it waiting?"

That was like Frank, Rod thought. No amount of trouble ever bothered him for more than a few seconds.

"Go ahead." Rod reached for the beans. "Feed the critter. I oughta be like you, Frank. As long as a man can eat, he don't have no real trouble."

Doll dropped into the chair across from him. "Trouble's on the way, Rod, big trouble. Everybody in town's talking about it. They say

Hermann isn't coming to the valley just for the ride."

"Forget it," Frank said. "We don't have nothing he wants."

But Rod had something Jason Abbot wanted. Or someone else, if it wasn't Abbot. Rod began to eat, worry gnawing at his mind again. He thought about Kane's notion that George was back of the accidents, and he wondered if he knew his brother as well as he thought he did. A man could change with the years, especially when he worked for a millionaire like Karl Hermann, who dominated everything around him.

Doll brought the pie to the table and cut it, glancing at him often, the little smile he knew so well clinging to her lips. She was up to something, he thought, and was afraid to guess what it was. Anything could happen when she was in one of her crazy moods, especially with Frank here to encourage her.

When Rod finished his piece of pie, he leaned back in his chair and rolled a smoke. "Good pie," he said. "Be sure and thank your ma for it."

Doll jumped up pretending she was furious. "Rod Devers, is that pie the only good thing you just ate?"

"Make him eat a biscuit!" Frank yelled. "Choke him till he says it's good."

Doll grabbed a biscuit from the plate and before Rod knew what she was going to do, she was on his lap, trying to shove the biscuit into his mouth.

"Is it good?" she demanded.

He spluttered, twisting his head and trying to push her off his lap, but she clung to him, her face within a foot of his. The biscuit crumbled in her hand and she threw what was left on the floor.

"I'll get you another one!" Frank shouted. "Don't let him up."

"Never mind," she said, and, putting her hands on the sides of Rod's face, kissed him on the mouth. She drew her head back, asking: "Did that taste as good as Ma's pie?"

"A lot sweeter," he said. "You don't have to shove a biscuit at me just to get a kiss."

"I'm entertaining Frank." She waved at him. "The show's over. Go on home."

"Nothing doing," Frank said. "I brought you here, so I've got to take you back."

"I'm not going till morning." Doll rubbed the tip of her nose against Rod's. "It'll be daylight then and I can go by myself."

Frank scratched his head, not sure whether Doll was serious or not. "Why don't you marry the girl, Rod?"

"I'm going to," Rod said.

Doll put the side of her face against his chest, the top of her head coming under his chin. She whispered: "Tomorrow, Rod. At high noon."

Rod was silent, holding her that way for a

90

time. He couldn't say anything without starting a quarrel and he didn't want to do that. The last quarrel would do for the rest of his life. Now he had the terrible feeling that Doll could not be put off any longer, that she had come out here tonight to make that clear.

In a sudden burst of violence, Doll tore herself free from Rod's embrace and jumped up. "How about you marrying me, Frank? I just got turned down."

"Doll, it's not that . . . ," Rod began.

Frank was standing in the doorway. He broke in: "You've got company, Rod."

Rod rose. "Maybe Kane's back to ask me again to go to that meeting."

The rider had pulled up outside, calling: "Hello the house!"

"Abbot," the girl breathed. "What's he doing out here?"

"You oughta make a good guess," Rod said, and walked to the door.

"Come in, Jason."

The horse trader walked up the path, his spurs jingling, and when Rod and Frank stepped back, Abbot came into the room. He was a tall, slender man who called himself a rancher and owned the Flying W, a small spread in the west end of the valley. But in reality ranching was a sideline with him. He spent most of his time in town, buying and selling horses and making loans to the small cowmen, and then watching the borrower with frantic concern until he repaid the loan.

Abbot always managed to be the best-dressed man in the valley. He wore a broad-brimmed black hat, a white shirt with a string tie, a Prince Albert, and tightly fitting riding britches. His boots, invariably polished until they held a high gloss, were imported from California. Abbot liked to brag that they were made by the best bootmaker on the Pacific Coast.

"Sit down and have a cup of coffee," Rod said. "Got some pie left."

"No thanks." Abbot's green eyes, as bright and sharp as splintered glass, were fixed briefly on Doll and then swung back to Rod's face. "Looks like I busted into something."

Doll stood stiffly beside the table. Frank moved back to the stove, his hands shoved into his pants pockets, and gave Abbot an unfriendly stare. Rod had heard some ugly gossip about Abbot and Doll's mother, and now it occurred to him that the man might have come here looking for Doll, although Rod could not think why he would.

"You ain't busting into anything." Rod pulled up a chair for Abbot. "Sit down."

"I'm not of a mind to visit," Abbot said, his gaze again flicking briefly to Doll's face. "You've heard about Karl Hermann coming to the valley?"

Rod nodded. "Everybody has, I reckon."

"We're scared, Devers . . . all of us," Abbot said. "I ain't ashamed to admit I am."

"Hermann can't touch you."

"You're wrong. He can touch all of us, and he will. You can depend on it he isn't coming here just to inspect Spade."

"Then why is he coming?"

"To see how much he can grab. I know something of his appetite for land, and I also know he has political connections which will enable him to clean all of us out of the valley if we don't fight."

"Let's wait and see what he aims to do."

Abbot shook his head. "I can't afford to wait. I propose to protect my interest and I'll go to any length to do it. That means money, but unfortunately most of my cash is loaned out. I came here tonight to ask you to let me have my two thousand by the end of the week. I'll forget the interest if . . ."

"Let's talk sense," Rod broke in. "The note isn't due for a couple of months."

Abbot's gaze swung to Doll again, her presence here obviously disturbing him. He cleared his throat and brought his eyes back to Rod's face. "Will you guarantee to pick up your note when it's due?"

"When I borrowed the money, you said . . ."

"I know, I know," Abbot said impatiently, "but at the time I had no idea Karl Hermann was coming. I will not be run out of this valley, Devers. If I have to recruit an army to stay, that's what I'll do." He cleared his throat again. "I'll expect that money the First of September."

Rod struggled with his temper, fighting the impulse to drive a fist into Abbot's smug face. He said: "You know I've got some four-year-old steers I was counting on selling, but by the time I drive to Winnemucca . . ."

"I don't want excuses," Abbot said crisply. "I want the interest and principal paid when the note's due, or I'll take steps."

"You want the heifers?"

Abbot shook his head. "You paid twice what they were worth. I want cash, Devers."

Rod stared at Abbot's cold face that was without the slightest hint of friendly intent. Rod's temper, already pulled thin by the things that had happened the last few hours, suddenly snapped. He started toward Abbot, convinced that the horse trader, for some malicious reason of his own, was determined to smash everything Rod had worked three years to build.

"Take it easy!" Frank shouted at Rod. "Beating him up won't pay off no note."

"That's right." Abbot had drawn a small gun from his pocket. "Stay where you are, Devers. I didn't come here to fight. As a matter of fact, I'm doing you a favor by letting you know exactly where you stand."

Rod stopped a step from the man, breathing hard, his eyes on the gun. "You probably figure that stripping my range is doing me a favor. And mudding up my spring and busting my fences are more favors." He motioned to the door. "Get out before I take that popgun away from you and break your damned neck."

"You wouldn't break my neck with a hole in your brisket, Devers. But I've said what I came to say, so I'm ready to go." Abbot nodded at Doll. "I'll take you home."

"You won't take me anywhere, Abbot," the girl breathed.

"I can't leave you here with these men," Abbot said harshly. "I think enough of your good name to look out for you."

"You dirty coyote." Frank moved toward Abbot, his big hands fisted at his sides, the habitual good humor gone from his face. "Put that gun up. When I get done with you, you'll be eating them words, along with a few teeth."

Abbot wheeled to face Frank, lining the gun on him. "I know what'll happen if I don't get her out of here. Unless she goes with me, I'll see that everyone in the valley knows she spent the night here."

Rod lunged at him. Abbot jumped back and fired, but his attention had been fixed on Frank and he was slow and panicky. Rod grabbed his right wrist and twisted it until the gun fell to the

95

floor. He yanked the man around and kicked him in the seat, and Abbot went headlong through the door. He stumbled across the porch and sprawled into the dirt of the yard.

"You open your mug about Doll and I'll blow your teeth through the back of your head. You savvy, Abbot?"

The horse trader got to his feet and turned, the lamplight falling across his narrow, bitter face.

"There's something you'd better savvy, Devers. I have a good memory." Turning, Abbot crossed the yard to his horse and mounted.

Rod stood in the doorway until the sound of hoofs had died downslope, then he reached for his gun belt and took it down from a peg on the wall. He buckled it around him, and when he looked up, he saw that Doll had dropped into a chair at the table.

"I'm sorry, Rod," she said miserably. "He spoiled everything. He must have got out of Ma where I was."

He stared at her, realizing that she was trying to say Abbot had used the note as an excuse to come here tonight, that it was really Doll's presence which had brought him—but that didn't make sense. Rod knew he had Doll's mother's approval. Whatever Abbot had done or whatever purpose he'd had was entirely his and not Doll's mother's.

"It's all right," Rod said. "Abbot didn't do no harm."

"He will," Doll whispered. "You don't know him. Nobody knows him but me and Ma. He's the only man I ever met who makes me feel undressed just by meeting his eyes." She rose. "Go saddle your sorrel, Rod. I'll clean up the dishes."

"I might as well get along," Frank said.

Rod left the cabin with Frank, and when they were outside, he said: "Looks like we've got trouble, all right, but it ain't none of Karl Hermann's doing."

"Go put your iron back," Frank said in a low tone. "Toting it won't do nothing but fetch trouble."

"Then I guess I'll just help fetch it, Frank," Rod said.

"But, damn it, you're doing just what Abbot wants you to!" Frank shouted. "Can't you see that?"

"You're talking to the wrong boy, Frank. Save your wind."

"You can't meet a note with lead."

"And a dead man can't collect a note."

"Oh, hell," Frank muttered, and was silent.

Neither said anything until Rod's sorrel was saddled. They walked to the hitch rack, Rod leading his animal.

He said: "I may stay in town tonight. Kane's

having a meeting to fight Hermann. I might stick my nose into it long enough to find out what they're up to."

"They didn't ask me," Frank said sourly.

Rod could have told him that Kane had no respect for him and had purposely overlooked him because he didn't want him at the meeting, but there was nothing to be gained by telling him. Frank would know anyhow, if he wanted to be honest with himself.

"You're lucky," Rod said. "Wish he hadn't mentioned it to me."

Frank stepped into his saddle and sat looking down at Rod. He asked hesitantly: "Was it all right to bring Doll out from town? She asked me to."

"Sure," Rod said. "I was going into town to see her in a day or two anyhow."

"I'll ride over tomorrow night," Frank said. "Just to see what you found out about Kane's meeting. So long."

"So long," Rod said.

He remained outside for a time, listening to the beat of Frank's horse's hoofs until the sound was lost to the east. He wished he could skip the next hour or two, for he knew what Doll would say. But he could not change his decision about postponing their wedding. Abbot's visit had made him even more sure that he was right, but Doll would insist he was just being stubborn.

Finally it would reach a clash of wills, and if he lost her . . . He shook his head. Nothing would be worse than that, but for Doll's good, he could not give in to her. He walked to the cabin, knowing that Doll would laugh in his face if he told her it was for her own good. She would tell him she knew better than anyone else what was good for her.

When he went in, she had finished washing and drying the dishes and was putting them away. She glanced over her shoulder at him, smiling briefly.

"I hate working in Ma's hotel," she said, "but there's nothing I'd rather do than work for you."

He crossed the room to her and took her hands. "Please listen to me, Doll. From the time I was a little kid I've wanted to own a spread. That was why I did things I'm ashamed of now, but it was the only way I could make any quick money outside of robbing a bank."

She squeezed his hands. "I know that, Rod, and I want to help you."

"I know you do," he said. "Having supper ready when I get home, and well . . . just having you here, is something I want more than anything else. But I'm in trouble, Doll. You saw that tonight. Let's put off getting married till I'm out of debt."

"Just wait and wait and wait." She shook her head. "I'm not good at waiting, Rod. I love you so. We were going to get married in the spring, and then June. Well, June's about gone."

"We talked it over," he said, "about buying those heifers. Now I can see I was the biggest idiot in Oregon, but I couldn't then. And borrowing from Abbot to boot." He shook his head. "No use cussing myself over something I've already done. What I've got to worry about is raising two thousand dollars. And when I do, we'll get married."

"Rod, I won't quarrel with you again. I'm sorry about the things I said the last time you were in town. Since then I've . . . I've made up my mind. It's tomorrow, or not at all."

She dropped his hands and put her arms around him, the side of her face against his shirt.

He said: "I've seen too many women marry men who couldn't support them. Like Todd Shannon's wife."

"Don't compare yourself to a no-good like Todd Shannon," she cried. "We'll make out."

"Not if we had a family," he said, tight-lipped. "Not even if there was just you and me, and Abbot took my cattle, which it looks like he will. Wait a little longer, Doll . . . just till fall."

She stepped away from him and walked across the room to where she had hung her hat from a set of antlers. She swung back to face him, jamming her hat on her head. "You've got two loves, Rod . . . the Rocking R and me . . . and the Rocking R was in your heart a long time before I was."

"It don't mean I love you any less because . . ."

"That's where you're wrong. I suppose it's a good thing I saw it in time. I won't come second to a ranch. I'm first or I'm nothing."

"Oh, hell. You and the Rocking R are two different things. A man don't love his wife like he does his ranch."

"Yes, we're different things," she said brightly. "I'd cook for you and patch your clothes and clean your cabin. I'd sleep with you at night and keep you warm and give you pleasure. Not like Ma and Abbot, but . . ."

She whirled and ran outside.

So the gossip was true, Rod thought. He blew out the lamp and closed the door, and when he reached the hitch rail, Doll was already in the saddle.

"I shouldn't have said it," she whispered. "It's just that I'm haunted by the feeling that if we were married now, we could be happy, but if we wait, we'll lose our chance. I'm afraid of Abbot, Rod. I'm terribly afraid."

Looking up at her face, a faint oval in the starshine, he sensed that she was giving him this last chance. Still, he could not change. She was in no danger from Abbot, and what Abbot and her mother did was their business. If Rod got out of debt by fall, they could get married. If he went under, she was better off to be free of him.

"When a man has any pride, Doll," he said

101

slowly, "he wants to take care of his wife. But if he's broke, just working for his thirty a month and beans, he can't. Then his pride . . ."

"Pride," she cried. "Say that word one more time and I'll . . . I'll . . ."

She didn't finish. She wheeled her horse around and started downslope toward town.

Rod stepped into the saddle and caught up with her. They hadn't quarreled this time, not the way they had before, but they were finished. Perhaps it was better to cut it off with one quick stroke than to keep gnawing at it and making themselves unhappy.

He looked up at the sky, the stars glittered like cold, brilliant jewels, and he knew that he was trapped. He was wrong if he married Doll tomorrow . . . if he didn't, he'd lose her.

Neither Rod nor Doll felt like talking on their way into town. Rod's thoughts were a sour stream in his mind. He tried to focus his mind on Jason Abbot, tried to figure out why Abbot was so determined to break him. At least the man had come into the open.

Only a miracle could prevent three years of hard work and hope from being lost. Rod was not sure he could start over. He had seen men broken and twisted by hard luck until they were no good to themselves or anyone else. The realization that he had no one to blame but himself didn't help. He had got himself into debt because he was in too big a hurry to get where he wanted to be. What had looked like a good gamble last spring had turned out to be a bad one. But Doll was the big loss, not the Rocking R.

He glanced at her, realizing that no matter how hard he tried to put her out of his mind, his thoughts always returned to her. What had been a mere ambition in his boyhood had taken on real meaning because of Doll. But she wouldn't, or couldn't, understand that. Resentment rose in him then. If she was breaking it off just because she wasn't getting her way, he didn't want her for his wife. But he was rationalizing, finding excuses for himself, and it didn't help.

The country tipped down for three miles below Rod's cabin, then it leveled off. The road followed Egan Creek. Once it had finished its brawling passage out of the Blue Mountains, it became a slowly moving stream, meandering across the valley to flow into Egan Lake another two miles beyond Poplar City.

Now, with the lights of the town directly before them, Rod said: "Thanks for coming out and cooking supper."

"You're welcome," Doll said crisply.

He was silent until they reached the first outlying houses of the town, lamplight bright in their windows, and then he broke down his pride enough to say: "You busted it off, Doll, but maybe it'll make you feel good to know I'll

103

always love you. There'll never be anyone else."

She laughed shortly. "Not till the next time a wind lifts some skirt enough for you to see a pretty ankle, if there are any pretty ankles in Egan Valley besides mine."

She was breaking it off all right, clean and sharp, and she was working herself into a rage so she could do it right.

He was angry then, and when they reached the hotel, he said: "Tell your ma I'll need a room tonight, but don't think I'm staying on the chance of seeing you again."

"That's just fine, because I never want to see you again as long as I live." Doll dismounted and handed the reins to Rod. "Put my horse up."

He hesitated, hating her at that moment, and, then he thought how silly this was. You didn't really love a woman if you got so angry at her you thought you hated her, so he didn't hate her and he never would.

"Sure, I'll take care of him," he said.

She looked up at him, standing so that the light from the hotel lobby touched the side of her face. He saw the hurt and the misery that was so clearly shown there, and wondered what she was seeing in his face.

She must have realized she was letting him see her feelings. She cried: "Go poke your head in a horse trough." Then she whirled quickly and ran into the lobby.

He rode on down the street to the livery stable, leading Doll's horse. When he came back through the archway a moment later, he considered going into the Palace. The best thing that could happen to him would be to get into a hell of a good fight. But chances were he couldn't rig up a fight just now when he wanted one. Well, he'd get a drink, anyhow.

A long line of horses stood racked in front of the saloon, and suddenly he remembered Sam Kane's meeting. He shrugged and moved along the walk to the hotel. To hell with the meeting. Feeling the way he did now, he might get his fight and wind up killing the wrong man. Better stay out of it, he decided, and stepped into the lobby.

He crossed the lobby to the desk, feeling the stagnant heat that the room still harbored from the warm day. He touched the brim of his hat, saying to Doll's mother who was behind the desk: "Howdy, Marcia."

"Good evening, Rod." She had a special tone of voice for him that he never heard her use on any other man, one of several ways she had of showing him that she favored him for a son-in-law. "Doll said you'd be in. You can have Room Twelve. It's on the front corner, cooler than the others."

"Thanks," he said, and waited for her to give him the key.

But she was in no hurry. She stood with her hands on the desk, blue eyes on him in a searching stare that seemed to probe his mind. He knew, then, that Doll had told her mother what had happened.

"How does it feel to have a girl want to marry you tomorrow, and have to turn her down?" Marcia asked.

"Like hell. I forgot to fetch your pie pan back."

He didn't want to discuss Doll. He shifted his weight uneasily, not knowing what to expect. He liked and respected Marcia Nance. When he had come to the valley, she had just started operating the hotel, and the talk was that Jason Abbot had put up most of the money. Those who were inclined to gossip made a good deal of it, but true or not it didn't make Rod think any the less of her.

She was surprisingly young to have a grown daughter, and she was handsome in a mature way that Doll had not yet achieved. Her hair was darker than Doll's, although in the light of the bracket lamp above her it seemed definitely red. There was a close resemblance between Doll and her mother, and now, meeting Marcia's gaze, Rod was more aware of it than ever. In another fifteen years Doll would look exactly as Marcia looked now.

"Have you got time to talk, Rod?" Marcia asked.

He looked down at the desk, frowning, then he said: "Sure."

"We'll go back into the parlor," she said, "but you'd better step into the bar. Pablo Sanchez rode into town about an hour ago. He was looking for you, and I told him you'd be in."

"I don't want to see Pablo," Rod said.

She shrugged. "I'll tell him, but I'll die of curiosity, wondering what he wanted."

Sanchez was one of Karl Hermann's *vaqueros*. He had come north with George Devers when Hermann had sent George to Spade, and now he was George's *segundo*. Most of the former crew had stayed on, several of them Mexicans who had come to the valley with Clay Cummings when he had started Spade. After Cummings had sold out, he had asked Hermann to keep the crew.

Rod, thinking of this now, remembered what Sam Kane had said about George's being back of the accidents that had pestered him for so long. He wondered if there could be some connection between the accidents and Sanchez's presence in town.

Marcia had started toward the bar. Rod caught up with her, saying: "I'll see what Sanchez wants." Then he went on through the door that opened into the bar.

Sanchez was playing solitaire at one of the poker tables, his sombrero on the other side of the cards. When he saw Rod, he picked up his sombrero and rose, a quick smile making a flash of white against the swarthy background of his skin.

"Missus Nance say you will be along, *amigo*," Sanchez said, "so I wait."

"She said you wanted to see me."

Sanchez nodded, still smiling. "The boss wants you to come to Spade. He sent me to get you."

"Nothing to keep George from riding my way," Rod said brusquely.

Sanchez spread his hands. "But already the smell of trouble is in the air. *Señor* Devers says he might start it if he rode into town."

"What kind of trouble?"

Sanchez shrugged. "*¿Quien sabe?* It is in the air like a bad stink in your nose. We do not want it, *amigo*, but it is there."

"I've got trouble enough of my own without taking on some of Spade's."

"But we are all together. *Señor* Devers says his brother can help."

The impulse was in Rod to say no and walk out, but he hesitated, considering this thing which was so utterly unexpected. He had never known George to ask for help from anyone, to ask it from his brother was almost unbelievable. Sanchez probably knew what George had in mind, but Rod was sure the *vaquero* would say nothing more.

Because his curiosity was stirred, Rod said: "I'll be out in the morning."

Sanchez nodded, smiling again. *"Bueno."*

Returning to the lobby, Rod saw that Marcia was not behind the desk. As he hesitated, Doll came out of the dining room. She said with cool indifference: "Why don't you go to bed?"

Rod had learned a long time ago that Doll's mood could swing from one extreme to the other in a short space of time. She appeared utterly composed, and now, standing a few feet from her, it seemed to Rod that they were complete strangers.

Matching her cool tone, he said: "Your ma wanted to talk."

"Nothing to talk about." He saw the familiar sparkle of deviltry in her eyes as she added: "Go to bed. Maybe by morning you'll get around to thinking what it would be like if I was your wife."

He forced a smile, and, reaching out, put a fingertip against her nose. "Why didn't that grow?"

She jumped back. "I'll push your nose right out through . . ."

But he didn't stay to find out where she was going to push his nose. He walked rapidly down the hall to Marcia's parlor in the rear of the building. The door was open and he saw that

Marcia was sitting in her rocking chair, some sewing on her lap.

She said—"Come in, Rod,"—and went on with her sewing.

Rod stepped into the room and closed the door. "George sent for me." He dropped into a leather chair on the other side of the oak table. "I'm going out to Spade in the morning."

She glanced up. "What does your brother want?"

He sensed a wariness in her that seemed out of place. He said: "Sanchez didn't say." There was an awkward silence while he rolled a smoke, then he asked: "How did you know I'd be in town tonight?"

"I knew you wouldn't let Doll ride in by herself." Marcia put her sewing down. "Doll told me you'd broken off. You're a strong-willed man, Rod. Sometimes you're filled with so much stubbornness and pride that you don't have room for anything else."

He had not come here to hear Marcia discuss his faults. He reached for a match, saying bluntly: "Did you ever think that your daughter might have the same trouble?"

Marcia smiled. "I certainly have. In some ways you're a lot alike."

"And did it ever occur to you that maybe I love her so much I won't marry her while I'm up to my neck in trouble and debt?" he asked harshly.

"Yes, it has, Rod." She pointed to the gun on his hip. "Doll said Jason Abbot had been out there, but why . . . ?"

"If she told you about Abbot, you know why I'm wearing it."

"Yes, I . . . I guess I know." She folded her hands on her lap and rocked steadily for a moment, the only sound in the room the squeak of the chair under her. Then she asked: "Rod, what is it you want more than anything else in the world?"

"My own outfit. I've wanted that since I was a kid. After Hermann's bank took our spread, I knew I had to do it alone. I reckon that's why I'm in this jam, starting without enough and borrowing from Abbot."

"Then it's like Doll told you. The Rocking R is your first love."

He struck the match and lighted his cigarette, staring at Marcia through the smoke, angry because she had trapped him. He said: "No, it's not like that. I won't marry her till I can take care of her."

"I see." Marcia continued to rock, a pulse beat in her temple a steady throbbing. "I'm sure you've heard the gossip about Jason and me. I won't deny it. I won't even defend myself, except to say that I haven't had an easy life. Doll was born when I was sixteen. Since then there have been times when I wasn't sure she'd have anything to eat from one meal to the next, and times when I didn't.

"Listen to me, Rod. I want the best for Doll, so I'd like to help you. I have a little influence with Jason. I'll talk to him if you'll let me."

"No. I've never got behind a woman's skirt and I won't now."

"You're too stubborn and proud," she said. "I'm sorry. I thought it was one way I could avert the trouble that's coming."

"What do you know about the trouble that's coming?"

She rose and walked to the window and stood there, a hand gripping the chintz curtain, her body rigid. "I know all about it. I hate Jason and I hate myself. It's like a bog. You take one wrong step and it sucks you in."

Rod rose. "No need to hurt yourself talking like this, Marcia."

"Wait. I've got to tell you because I'm the only one who knows." She turned to him, her face pale. "Jason is . . . well, he's crazy. I've seen him walk around this room for half an hour at a time, snapping his fingers and hitting himself on the chest and shouting that the day will come when he'll be a bigger man than Karl Hermann. That's what's back of all this talk about trouble. He has money . . . quite a bit of it . . . and in a roundabout way he's done all he can to stir up a fight."

"He must be crazy to think he can lick a man like Hermann."

"Possessed is a better word . . . possessed by an evil spirit. He knows how Hermann got his start, how everything he touched turned to money, and he says he can do the same once he begins to grow. If Hermann was killed, his property would go to his daughter, and Jason thinks he could buy Spade cheap."

"He wouldn't murder Hermann."

"Yes, he would." She threw out her hands in a gesture of helplessness. "No one can stop him. He's worked hard to build up fear in Kane and the rest of them. It's made them crazy. You can do that with fear, you know, if you're sly and clever like Jason."

He found this hard to believe, for he had never thought of Jason Abbot as anything but a horse trader and a ten-cow rancher with a little money that he loaned out at a high rate of interest.

"Why is he putting the screws on me?" Rod asked.

"He's afraid of you because you're the one man in the valley he can't influence. You might be able to turn the others against him. He's spent hours talking about Hermann's cruelty and greed, and he keeps reminding Kane and the others that George is Hermann's man. You're George's brother, and that makes you Jason's enemy."

So Abbot had been back of the things Sam Kane

had said that afternoon. Rod asked: "Abbot's been causing my bad luck?"

She nodded. "He knows that a man like you can be broken by constant pressure, but not by a single threat."

Marcia walked back to her rocking chair and sat down. Rod, watching her, realized how much worry was in her, the tragic sense of hopelessness, and he knew it was Doll's future which bothered her.

"You don't really think you could change Abbot's mind about collecting that note, do you?" Rod asked.

"I might be able to persuade him to make you a fair offer for your cattle if you'd leave the country."

"I wouldn't take it."

"No, I suppose you wouldn't." She took a long breath. "There's one thing you haven't learned, Rod. A man can't live alone. Jason will see to it that you lose every friend you have in the valley but Frank Benson. What will you do then?"

"Put a slug in Jason."

"And Sam Kane and his bunch will lynch you." She hesitated, and then as Rod moved to the door, she said: "Don't tell anybody what I told you about Jason. We can't really prove anything."

He paused, one hand on the knob, his eyes on her bleak face. He sensed a bitterness in her that he'd never felt before, and it surprised him, for he had always found her a pleasant woman, given to joking and easy laughter. But tonight she had let him have a glimpse of her tortured soul, and he wondered if there was more to this than she had told him.

"I ain't a blabbermouth, Marcia," he said.

"I know you're not," she said quickly, and then as he opened the door, she added: "We're going to have terrible trouble, Rod. If you love Doll, you'll marry her and take her away from here. Anywhere. I'll stake you to a start somewhere else."

"I can't do it," he said, and left the room.

When he went through the lobby, he saw with relief that Doll was not behind the desk. He paused outside on the walk and smoked a cigarette, thinking that whatever trouble was coming would not affect Doll, and probably not Marcia. But why had she been so anxious for him to get out of the country?

He threw his cigarette away with a sudden, violent gesture, finding no answer to the question, and crossed the street to the Palace. He would be perfectly happy, he thought gloomily, if there were no women in the world.

Rod's only purpose in going into the saloon was to find out what had come of Kane's meeting. When he pushed through the batwings, he saw the men at the bar turn and look at him and then give him their backs, all but old Clay Cummings at the end of the bar. He remembered Marcia Nance saying: *Jason will see to it that you lose every friend in the valley but Frank Benson.*

In that moment he had glimpsed the dark and barren quality on the faces of his neighbors, their hostility flowing toward him like a blast of chill air. These were men he had known for three years. He had ridden roundup with them spring and fall and once a year had helped drive a pooled-together herd to the railroad at Winnemucca.

Old Clay Cummings stood alone at the bar, a craggy-faced white-headed eagle of a man. Rod walked to him and stood beside him, motioning to the bartender who brought a bottle and a glass.

Rod said: "Howdy, Clay. How are you?"

"If you're asking about my health, it ain't good. Ever see a nightmare, Rod? See it start little and grow big until it looks like a pink cow twenty feet tall . . . the kind you see when you're drunk?"

"No," Rod said. "Have a drink with me, Clay?"

Cummings said: "Why not. Maybe we'll see a few pink cows."

"Not today," Rod said. "This ain't the time."

Cummings shrugged his bony shoulders. "Dunno about that. One time looks as good as another to me."

Rod filled the glasses and they lifted them and drank. Cummings ran the back of a hairy hand across his mouth and putting his hand on the bar again, began nudging the shot glass back and forth between thumb and forefinger. He had been the first real settler in the valley, coming in the late 1860s when the Paiutes were a constant menace and the only other whites within fifty miles were the soldiers at Camp Harney.

Cummings had settled between the lakes on Halfmile Creek, where he had built a big white house and furnished it extravagantly. He had bought fifty thousand acres of swampland from the state. He had claimed all the valley and seventy miles of grassland to the south along the Steens Mountains.

At one time Cummings had been worth half a million, but then his luck had turned sour, largely because he couldn't keep from going to California every summer and betting on horse races. Once he got into debt he had not been able to come back, so he had borrowed repeatedly from the banks. Finally he had been forced to sell to Karl Hermann, salvaging nothing from his empire but a small ranch on the east side of the Steens, fifty miles to the south.

Cummings said: "You ain't popular with this crowd, Devers. Sam Kane separated the sheep from the goats tonight, and you're a goat."

"No place in between, I reckon," Rod said.

"Not for them that's in the valley. Funny thing the way men get boogered till they run like stampeding steers. They'll go right over a rim once they get going. I recollect, once a storm started a herd of mine to stampeding and I lost every damned head."

"Anybody trying to turn these boys?"

"Wouldn't be no use. I've been standing here listening to Sam tonight. Loco, just plain loco. Shoot Hermann on sight, he says. Otherwise, they'll get cleaned out. You don't get big like he done and be honest, Sam says. Only difference between Hermann and a common rustler is size."

"He's partly right, just partly," Rod said.

Cummings stroked his white beard, faded blue eyes fixed on Rod's face. "Not even partly, sonny. Hermann is smart and he never misses a chance to make a dollar, but that ain't the same as being crooked."

Rod didn't argue. He'd heard George say the same thing about Hermann, and now he began to wonder if he had been wrong all these years and George had been right. It was not a pleasant thought.

He stared down at the shiny surface of the cherry-wood bar, unaware that Todd Shannon had come to stand beside him until the man said: "You should have been here tonight, Devers."

Startled, Rod glanced up. Shannon was his neighbor to the west, a furtive, lazy man who neglected his wife and children and lost more cattle every winter than any other rancher in the valley. Still he always had money for poker or whiskey. It was a puzzle that no one had been able to explain.

"Reckon you were here with bells on, Todd," Rod said.

"You're damned right. What Sam says makes sense. We hit first or we're licked. Hermann's got a bunch of outlaws on Spade. And when he gets here, he'll run us over the hill. He's done it on every range wherever he got a toehold."

"Sounds like Sam," Rod said.

"Talk," Cummings snorted. "Just fool talk. Why, them boys on Spade worked for me. Most of 'em, anyhow. Ain't an outlaw in the bunch."

Shannon blew out a long breath, the tips of his sweeping mustache quivering. "Easy enough for you to say, Clay, living where you do and being a bachelor, but most of us have a wife and kids, and, by hell, we'll fight for 'em."

"Ever try working for 'em?" Cummings asked truculently.

"You on Hermann's side?" Shannon demanded.

"I ain't on nobody's side," the old man snapped. "I just want to get along, but this crazy business tonight ain't gonna do nobody no good."

"Abbot here?" Rod asked.

"Got in for the tail end of the meeting," Shannon said. "Didn't have much to say. He's in the back room now with Sam. Chuck England and Barney Webb are with 'em." He cleared his throat, giving Rod a characteristic, sidelong glance. "Was I you, Devers, I'd just dust along."

"I ain't quite ready," Rod said irritably.

"Just thought I'd tell you," Shannon muttered, and walked away.

"Damned old woman," Cummings said. "Never did like a man who could walk up on you without being heard like that gent can."

"Just what did they do tonight?"

"Organized what they're calling the Ninety-Nine," Cummings said. "Sam's the head of it. Him and Abbot and that beanpole of an Otto Larkin are what they call an executive committee."

"They decide anything?"

"They gave this committee power to decide things." Cummings shook his head. "I'm out of it, being so far south, but it's bad business. Murdering Karl Hermann won't fetch 'em nothing but trouble."

Suddenly the door of the back room was flung open and Sam Kane walked out. Abbot followed, then Rod saw England and Webb, Abbot's men who worked on his ranch and handled the horses that he traded for. Both were wearing guns. Rod was startled, for it was the first time since he had come to the valley that he had seen a man carry a gun, except an occasional drifter who had been riding through the country.

Kane saw Rod and moved toward him, his big face more flushed than usual. Abbot and his men remained in the rear of the room, but Todd Shannon and Otto Larkin and the others who had been at the bar now swung in behind Kane, forming a solid line as they tacitly accepted his leadership.

"I told you how it was this afternoon," Kane said in a loud, ringing voice as if he felt a current of power generated by the knowledge that he had a crowd at his back. "You didn't come to the meeting."

"Why, I guess I didn't," Rod said mildly.

"We're organized now," Kane said, the burden of importance a heavy weight upon him. "I aim to see to it that Hermann hears that as soon as he gets to the valley."

"I reckon that'll scare him right back over the pass," Rod murmured.

Kane took a long breath, his face getting redder. "You don't need to hooraw me, Devers. We ain't gonna sit around and get knocked over one at a time." He motioned to the men behind him. "I want these boys to hear what you told me this afternoon, that you ain't having nothing at all to do with us in the future."

Kane had worked himself into a high rage, the color of his face deepening until it was more purple than red. Even the fold of fat on the back of his neck above his coat collar had taken on that same purplish hue.

"That ain't what I said, Sam." Rod was annoyed

by Kane's attitude. "I say you're a damned fool to kick up a lot of dust before you know with certainty there's any reason for it."

"I'm a damned fool! Well, you're a bigger damned fool than I am because you're trying to straddle the fence. We won't let you. Which is it? Are you on our side or Hermann's?"

"If you're right about Hermann, I'm on your side. But I aim to find out first."

Kane swung to face the others. "If you're right, he says. Hell, we know we're right. Likewise we know he's George Devers's brother and we know he had a talk with that Mex Sanchez tonight. I guess we know enough, don't we?"

They nodded, Larkin saying ominously: "We ain't standing for no traitor living north of Spade."

Kane made a slow turn to face Rod again.

Then it came to Rod what they planned to do and he could see Jason Abbot's hand behind it. The horse trader wasn't waiting until the 1st of September. They wouldn't be satisfied with giving him a whipping. They aimed to run him out.

"We'll show you what we do to traitors," Kane said, and started toward Rod.

Abbot had left, but England and Webb were still in the back of the room. The line behind Kane moved with him. Rod, looking past Kane at these men who were his neighbors, knew that

Marcia had been right. He didn't have a friend among them. They were a pack of wolves intent on pulling down the man who refused to run with them.

Clay Cummings still stood behind Rod and to his left. He had not moved; he had not said anything. There was no doubt about the old man's solid courage, and there could be no doubt about his feeling toward Sam Kane and his bunch. In that moment Rod made his decision. He unbuckled his gun belt and, wheeling, handed it to Cummings.

"Keep 'em off my back, Clay," Rod said. "I don't aim to fight all of 'em."

Cummings grabbed the belt, yanked the gun from holster, and laid the belt on the bar.

"All right, buckos!" he yelled. "If any of you horn into this, I'll let daylight into your guts. You back there . . . England . . . Webb. You savvy?"

Rod had swung around to face Kane, who had stopped, balancing himself on the balls of his feet. Kane had not expected this. He had counted on a dozen men backing his play. But now he knew he was alone, and he had worked himself into a position from which he could not escape without fighting.

Rod said: "I'm waiting, Sam. Show me."

Sam Kane cursed and jumped at Rod, right fist swinging for Rod's chin. Rod ducked and caught Kane on the nose with his left. It flattened under Rod's fist. Blood spurted, and the big man cried out in pain. He swung again. Rod stood his ground, taking Kane's blows on elbows and shoulders or rolling his head with each punch. He was the faster of the two. His co-ordination was better, and he kept pumping his left into Kane's face. They weren't hard blows, but they stung and cut, and in a matter of seconds Kane's face was a scarlet mask.

Suddenly Kane changed tactics. He fell forward, hands outstretched, and he got Rod by the legs and brought him down in a hard fall. Rod broke free and rolled away. As he got to his hands and knees and came on up to his feet, Kane reached out in a futile grab for an ankle.

Rod backed away, taunting: "Get up off the floor, Sam."

Cummings laughed. "You're kind of old to be playing down there, Sammy boy."

Kane was on his feet then, wiping a sleeve across his blood-smeared face. He lunged at Rod, his fists swinging. Again Rod stood his ground, cracking Kane in the stomach and in the face. For a time they stood there, trading blows, and there was no sound but the thudding of fists on bone and muscle and their panting struggle for breath. Then Kane landed an upswinging right to the side of Rod's face. Rod went down.

Pin-wheeling lights exploded across Rod's vision. Instinct made him roll cat-like. He caught the blur of Kane's big boot that missed his head by inches. He rolled again and got up and backed away, the yells of the watching men a crashing roar of sound against his ears.

He had to have time, and he gained it by continuing to back up, doing nothing but blocking Kane's blows while his head cleared. Kane, overanxious now, kept boring in, swinging uppercuts that never quite landed. Rod, still backing up, ran into a chair and sprawled over it, upsetting a table in his fall. Cards and chips spilled over him. Kane grabbed up the chair and threw it. Rod ducked it, for Kane was a little slow, and his one eye, almost closed, was bothering him.

Rod regained his feet, and taking the initiative, drove at Kane. He took a blow on the shoulder. He whipped a short, battering left into Kane's face that swiveled his head on his shoulders. He got Kane again on the cheek bone just in front of his ears, and Kane went down.

"Bust him, Devers!" Cummings yelled. "Damn him, give it to him in the guts!"

But Rod stood motionless, taking this moment to suck breath back into his tortured lungs. Kane struggled up to his hands and knees. He lifted his head and peered through his one good eye at Rod. Then he plunged forward, coming in low, his hands outstretched. Rod drove a knee into the man's face, the sound of the blow a sharp, ringing crack. Kane's head snapped back. He fell away and rolled over on his side and lay there, motionless, his mouth sagging.

For a moment the room pitched and turned before Rod, and from a great distance he heard Cummings say: "Larkin."

Rod lurched to the bar. He laid a hand on it and held himself upright, knowing he had been hurt more than he had realized.

Again Cummings shouted: "Damn you, Larkin, are you gonna make me kill you? Stand pat. Devers licked him fair enough."

"He killed him." The tall Larkin had moved out ahead of the others, bitter and vindictive. "If he did, we'll put a rope on his neck."

"He done what he had to," Cummings snapped. "He sure as hell didn't ask for this fight."

Rod reached for the gun belt and buckled it around his body. He wiped sweat and blood from his face. His breath was coming easier now.

He was able finally to say: "You follow Kane's lead and you'll fetch more trouble to this valley than you ever saw."

He backed toward Cummings, seeing that Kane was beginning to stir. He took his gun from Cummings's hand and went on out of the saloon. For a moment he leaned against the wall, the night wind sweet and cool against his battered face. He ran a tongue over his lips, tasting sweat and blood. His entire body was a great, aching mass of flesh. He opened and closed his hands and rubbed them against his legs. Then he went on along the boardwalk to the hotel.

Doll was at the desk when he reeled in, intent only on getting to his room. She cried: "What happened to you?"

He went on across the lobby to the foot of the stairs, then his knees folded and he fell on the stairs, his feet still on the floor.

"Ma!" Doll screamed. "Ma!"

Rod didn't lose consciousness, but he had the weird feeling he was standing to one side looking at himself. He heard running steps in the hall, and then Marcia's voice.

"What's wrong?"

"Rod." Doll pointed to him. "He looks like he got wound up in a buzz-saw."

Marcia saw him, and cried out involuntarily: "We've got to get him up to his room."

"Let's get the doc," Doll said.

"Can't. He's out at Larkin's place. Missus Larkin is having a baby."

Rod braced his hands against the stairs and pushed himself upright, Marcia and Doll holding his arms. Oddly, he thought of Larkin there in the saloon, when he should have been home with his wife.

"You've got to get up the stairs," Marcia said. "Try, Rod."

Somehow he did get up the stairs, both women partly lifting him and taking most of his weight. They turned him along the hall. Doll threw a door open and he went in and fell across the bed.

"Get some hot water and a rag," Marcia said, lighting a lamp. "He's hurt pretty bad."

"I'm all right," Rod muttered.

Marcia tugged his boots off. He got over on his back and unbuckled his gun belt by arching himself, pulled the belt out from under him, and dropped it beside the bed.

"Get Clay Cummings out of the saloon," he said. "Fetch him over here."

"He'll be all right," Marcia said. "Let's get your clothes off."

"I ain't so bad off I can't undress myself," he said. "Quit it."

"Deliver me from a stubborn man," Marcia breathed.

"Get out of here," he said. "I'll get my clothes off."

She went out and he heard Marcia say something to Doll. He sat up and pulled off his pants. He got out of his shirt and crawled under a quilt, exhausted by his effort.

Marcia came back in with a pan of hot water and a cloth. She wiped his face and examined the cuts.

"You'll have a scar or two out of this," she said. "You won't be so good-looking."

"Too bad." He tried to grin. "I sure was handsome."

"Who did it?"

"Kane."

"You hurt anywhere else?"

"No."

But he did hurt, his ribs and his chest and his belly, and each breath brought sharp pain. Just banged up, he thought, but he wasn't sure. He might have some broken ribs.

"I'll have the doctor look at you when he gets back," Marcia said, "and I'd better get word to Spade. You won't be riding out there in the morning."

"I figure I will," he said.

"Stubborn." She stood up, her hands on her hips. "Real stubborn."

He looked at her, managing a wry grin. "I work hard at it," he said. "Funny thing. I didn't know he was hurting me when we was fighting. Seemed like he got in just one real wallop and that one knocked me down."

"More than one." She sat down on the edge of the bed. "Was Jason there?"

"He left before the tussle." He saw that the corners of her mouth were trembling, and it surprised him, for she had always been a self-possessed woman who held her emotions under rigid control. "Forget it. Nothing to worry about."

"You don't know," Marcia said. "He's poisoned them . . . Kane and Larkin and all of them. I've heard him in the lobby talking to any of them he could get to listen. He'll use them and he doesn't care how many of them get killed. They won't listen, Rod. If you tell a lie often enough, folks believe you, and Jason has told it often. You've been neighbors to these men, but you don't understand them. You're different."

"No different. We all want to own our outfits and a two-bit herd." He reached out and took her hand. "Now quit worrying."

"No, you're different." She let her hand lie in his, her face quite plain now without the curve of the smile that usually touched the corners of her mouth. "You've never been a failure, Rod. These people have. It's their last chance. That's why Jason has been able to work on them. Well, I guess it's natural enough to be afraid of anyone as successful as Hermann."

He had never thought of it quite that way. She was probably right, for it could explain the panic that had turned them into a killer pack. Marcia turned her head and began to cry, and he squeezed her hand, saying: "It ain't your worry. Now quit it."

But he knew there was nothing he could say that would do any good. She was suffering an inner agony that he could not touch. She belonged to Jason Abbot, but she hated him, and she would

130

always hate him, and now she didn't know how to free herself.

Marcia rose. "I'm sorry, Rod," she murmured, wiping her eyes and turning to face him. "If there is anything a man hates, it's a bawling woman." She swallowed. "I'll kill him, Rod. Before this is done, I'll kill him." She turned to the door, then stopped and looked at him. "Rod, don't turn against Doll because of me. She's sweet and good. She deserves the best."

He searched for the right words to tell her that he respected her more than any woman he had ever known, that he would not hold her relationship with Jason Abbot against her. But it was a hard thing to say, and before he spoke, she was gone.

Clay Cummings came in a few minutes later, his Stetson in his hand, his long white hair brushed back from his forehead. He walked to the bed and looked down, a grudging admiration in his faded eyes.

"Quite a hassle, Devers," Cummings said. "Kane looks like he ran his face through a meat chopper. I wish I was young and full of vinegar like you are, but I'm old and licked. To hell with it."

"Kane all right?"

Cummings laughed. "He won't be all right for a week. Doll fetched me over."

"I wanted her to get you out of there. I was afraid they might take it out on you."

131

"No," he said derisively. "A wolf pack scatters after you knock the leader off, although Kane ain't much of a leader." He pulled at his beard, scowling. "You know, them boys bought a damned poor horse."

"Abbot's a horse trader," Rod said.

"I was thinking the same," Cummings said. "What's that ornery son up to?"

"He's got something up his sleeve," Rod said.

"And it ain't just his arm. Well, I'm going to bed."

"Blow out the lamp," Rod said.

Cummings nodded, walked to the bureau, and blew out the lamp. He went out, closing the door behind him. Rod lay there, his eyes closed, and presently he heard a band of riders leave town.

II

Rod slept better than he had expected to, and when he woke, it was broad daylight. He got up and washed, being careful not to disturb the wounds on his face. He was sore and stiff all over, and he still had a pain in his side when he breathed, but he felt better than he had hoped. He'd be able to ride.

He dressed and went downstairs to the dining room. Doll was waiting on a couple of drummers when he went in and sat down. Startled, she came to him.

"Rod Devers, you've got no business getting up . . ."

"I've got a lot of business to attend to." One side of his mouth was bruised and puffy, but the other side was good for a grin. "You're real pretty this morning."

She was angry at once, and started to say something, then checked it. "I suppose it's a compliment, coming from you." She wrinkled her nose at him. "I can't say the same for you."

"Don't do that."

"Do what?"

"Wiggle your nose. I can't count the freckles."

"I hate you."

"I'm glad to hear it. Ham and eggs, honey. I'm plumb empty."

She whirled and stalked back to the drummers' table, took their order, and went into the kitchen. She brought his plate of ham and eggs presently, and set a coffee cup beside it.

"Doc didn't get back last night. We were going to . . ."

"I'll be all right," he said, "soon as I get this grub inside me where it belongs."

"Rod, you aren't going . . ."

"You bet I am. Soon as I eat."

"You're tough, aren't you? You're a whole man and team and a dog under the wagon." She flounced back into the kitchen.

He ate, wondering about Frank Benson. But Frank wouldn't get hurt. He'd run. Nothing was very important to him.

When he finished eating, Doll was not in sight. He went into the lobby and found the desk deserted, so he left two silver dollars beside the register and went out into the sunlight.

It was warm even at this early hour, and he thought of the grass in his hay field that would be ready to cut in a few days. Probably the fence was down and Todd Shannon's cows were tromping the grass again. Well, it didn't make much difference. Not unless he could raise two thousand dollars by the 1st of

September—and he wouldn't make a bet on that.

He got his sorrel from the livery stable, paid the liveryman, and took the road to Spade. He held his horse down to a walk, for he found that the rocking motion sent pain knifing through his side. Half a mile from town he passed a sign that read: **Spade grass. If you don't have business on it, you're trespassing.**

Clay Cummings had put that sign up years ago, and George had left it, although there was no real reason for it to be there. The small ranchers had been satisfied to get along without antagonizing the one big layout in the valley.

The grass looked good. By late summer it would be belly-high on a horse. It had been an empty country when Clay Cummings had come north from California with his herd and Mexican *vaqueros*, and he had chosen well. The country here was floor-like, and in the late spring Egan Creek, fed by rain and melting snow in the Bluc Mountains, flooded the center of the valley. It was the best kind of natural irrigation, and Cummings had never lacked grass.

The road angled southeast, following a low ridge that bordered Egan Lake. Rod had made this ride once, shortly after he had come to the valley when Cummings, making his last desperate try to recoup his lost fortune, was holding on and hoping for a good beef price in the fall. But it hadn't come, and now, thinking

135

about the old man who had tamed this country, it seemed to Rod that there was no fairness about it.

Karl Hermann had taken advantage of Cummings's bad luck, just as he had taken advantage of Bill Devers's bad luck years before. The difference was that Rod's father had never been anything but a small rancher, so when Hermann's bank had taken his spread, it had gained nothing but a quarter-section of patented land and a water hole along with some graze that Bill Devers had used because no one else wanted it. But when Hermann bought Clay Cummings out, he'd bought an empire. There were at least ten thousand head carrying the Spade iron, and with proper management Hermann could double the number.

The lake stretched out before Rod, acres of tule marsh bordering it that was muskrats' heaven. Birds, too. Ducks, geese, swans, cranes, even the precious egrets that had brought fortunes for more than one transient hunter who had come here for them. Now, riding along the north edge of the marsh, another thought occurred to Rod. The tule marsh, drained and cleared, would make the best hay land in the world.

Hermann was a careful man, insisting that his ranchers carry hay from one year to the next so they would never be caught without a winter's supply. If Cummings had operated that way, he might not have been beaten, for his heavy winter losses had combined with low prices and his bad selection of race horses to whip him.

Rod reached the west edge of the lake and started across the dike that Cummings had built when he had first come to the valley. A sand reef lay to his left, holding back the waters of Egan Lake. If the reef ever went out, at least five thousand acres of what had been lake bottom would be exposed to the sun and might eventually be the home of fifty or more families. But the question of ownership was a knotty one and had been a subject of debate in the Palace and Marcia's hotel lobby for hours at a time.

Rod crossed the bridge that spanned Halfmile Creek, the slow-moving water making a liquid whisper of sound in the morning silence. A band of mallards flew over him, hitting the water of Egan Lake and skidding to a stop. A blue heron stood in the shallow water along the edge, motionless, stilt-legged. An avocet flew by, making the air melancholy with its cry.

Rod, riding up the sharp slope south of the lake, wondered if George liked it here, a strange country to a man raised on the dry Nevada rangeland. Rod shook his head, thinking he wouldn't swap his quarter-section on the mountain slope, with its pines and spring and view of the valley, for all of Spade.

When he rode into the ranch yard, he didn't notice any change: the sprawling white house shaded by tall poplars that Cummings had planted in the late 1860s, the huge barns and sheds built when nails were not available, their sides held together by rawhide, and the maze of stockade corrals that were peculiar to this country. They were made by setting juniper posts close together and threading willows between them, the strongest and longest-lasting corrals that could be made, according to Clay Cummings.

Thinking of the labor and hopes and dreams that had gone into the building of this ranch, Rod could not understand how Cummings had been able to take his loss as casually as he had. If the old man held any bitterness toward Karl Hermann, he hid it behind a mask of affability, saying he'd taken a licking and some-one else would have gobbled him up if Hermann hadn't.

Spade seemed to be deserted, although that seemed unlikely in view of the fact that George had sent for Rod. Then he heard someone banging an anvil in the blacksmith shop, and almost in the same instant an old Mexican came out of one of the barns. He moved toward Rod, who had dismounted and was watering his sorrel, his swarthy face creased by a toothy grin.

"*Saludos, amigo,*" the Mexican said. "*Señor* Devers is expecting you. Go in. I will care for your horse."

"Thanks, Juan," Rod said, recognizing the man.

He turned and walked along the row of poplars to the front door of the house.

The old Mexican was Juan Herrera, one of the few *vaqueros* still alive who had helped Clay Cummings drive his first herd to Egan Valley. When Cummings had made the sale to Hermann, he had stipulated that Juan was to be given a home on Spade as long as he lived. Actually he was receiving what amounted to a pension for past services. Now in failing health, nothing was required of him except a few easy chores around the barns and corrals.

It was an act of kindness on Hermann's part, a promise he could have easily forgotten once the transaction with Cummings had been completed. But he hadn't, and Juan was happy while he waited to die, content with a bunk and three square meals a day and the assurance he would be taken care of. Rod had never thought of it before, but now it struck him that Hermann had something in his makeup besides the love for wealth that seemed to dominate him so completely.

The door opened before Rod reached the porch and George stepped out, calling: "Glad you're here, boy! Didn't hear you ride up." He stopped, startled. "If I didn't know you were a good rider, I'd say your horse piled you into a juniper. What happened?"

"I tangled with Sam Kane last night."

George crossed the porch and held out his hand. "Well, I'm glad you got here, Rod. I was afraid you'd say to hell with it."

"I might have, if Marcia hadn't been curious about why Sanchez wanted to see me."

George frowned as if trying to identify Marcia. He was shorter than Rod and too pudgy for a man still in his early thirties. His eyes were gray, like Rod's, and his hair was very nearly the same medium brown except that he was getting a little bald in front, adding to his middle-aged appearance. There the resemblance ended. He had none of the quick grace, the long-boned lankiness, or the violent temperament that characterized Rod.

"Marcia," he said in a slow, thoughtful way, and then nodded as if finally remembering. "Missus Nance, the hotel woman?"

Rod nodded. "Sanchez was waiting for me in the bar and she sent me to see him."

"She's supposed to be Abbot's woman, isn't she?"

"So the gossips say," Rod said shortly, irritated by George's question.

"I know," George said. "I guess it's the same everywhere. People make a lot out of nothing. I know what they've done about Mister Hermann, and none of them know a damned thing about him." He swung toward the door. "Come in, Rod. No use standing out here in the sun."

The irritation in him growing, Rod followed George into the living room. George, he thought, was giving him a mild reprimand about his attitude toward Hermann. It rubbed him the wrong way, too, George always referring to his boss as "Mister Hermann."

Rod dropped into a leather chair just inside the door, knowing that the nagging pain in his side and the soreness which the ride had aggravated made him more edgy than usual. But he hadn't come here to quarrel with George. He put his hands on the arms and sat back, his gaze swinging around the room.

Everything about Spade was unusual, even this room. The mantel above the cavernous fireplace held a dozen brands belonging to the big outfits that lay south along the Steens and out into the desert toward Wagon Wheel country. The furniture was heavy and black, and thick drapes added to the gloom. The expensive Brussels carpet was dark blue. The room depressed Rod, and he wondered how George was able to live here.

"Like the room?" George asked.

"No."

"Didn't think you would." George sat down on a black leather couch. "I've left it the way it was, but if Grace doesn't like it, we'll change it."

"You mean this is the way Clay left it?"

"That's what I mean. He thought he was doing

everything up brown when he got this furniture and carpet. Cost a fortune." George drew a cigar from his coat pocket. "Fixed it up for his wife. You don't know the story?"

"No, never heard it."

"Clay thought his wife would come up here and live, but when the time came, she couldn't stand living in a wilderness with her nearest neighbor ten miles away." George shrugged. "Well, I guess nothing made much difference to Clay after that."

Rod nodded, thinking that it explained Clay Cummings's attitude. In one way he was like Juan Herrera—waiting to die. He had done a tremendous thing, bringing the first herd to the valley, but now, in the twilight of his life, it meant nothing to him.

Suddenly impatient, Rod asked: "What did you want me for?"

George took the cold cigar out of his mouth and stared at it, turning it slowly between his fingers. He said: "I've got no blood kin but you, Rod. I've been here for two years, and the only times I've seen you were when we met in town by accident. I'd like to change that."

George was not given to a show of emotion, and Rod had always supposed that their relationship was the way George wanted it. Even when George had come to the valley to visit him, they had found little to talk about. Later he had learned that George's real purpose in coming had been to make Cummings an offer for Spade, knowledge which had not made Rod think any better of him.

There was a tight moment of silence. Then Rod said: "I guess we ain't after the same thing."

"No, that was always the trouble." George looked up, the tip of his tongue touching dry lips. "You've always been a one-track man. You learned to handle a gun because you could make good money as a gunslinger and you wanted money to buy a ranch. As long as I can remember, the only thing you wanted was your own outfit."

"And you never did?"

George spread his hands. "I was satisfied to get on Karl Hermann's payroll. It's worked out pretty well for me. I've got one of the best jobs in his company."

George got up and walked to the door, his face troubled. It was the first time Rod had ever seen behind the mask of cool certainty that George habitually wore.

"Looks to me like you don't have a worry in the world," Rod said. "While I've got enough for both of us."

George leaned a shoulder against the door jamb, the cigar tucked between back teeth, his brooding eyes on Egan Lake.

After nearly a minute had passed, he said: "I've got more worries than you'd ever guess. Rod, has it occurred to you that you might be wrong about something?"

Surprised, Rod said: "Hell yes."

"I mean about Mister Hermann. You blamed him for taking Dad's spread, but afterward I found out he didn't even know about it. He owns five banks, and, as long as they're making a profit, he doesn't bother them."

A thought that had been nagging the back of Rod's mind took definite form. He had been like Sam Kane and the others, jumping to the conclusion that because a man had started with nothing and become a millionaire, he must be a thief. Kane's attitude had been ridiculous, wanting to fight before he knew whether he had any reason to. In the cool, depressing gloom of Spade's living room, Rod mentally admitted he had been as obstinate and stupid as Sam Kane and the others. He hadn't tried to find out anything, either. He only knew that Karl Hermann had owned the bank which had taken his father's place, therefore he had assumed that Hermann was responsible.

"Maybe it was that way," Rod said.

George wheeled to face him. "I never thought I'd hear you say that."

"I reckon Kane addled my brain." Rod grinned with the good side of his mouth. "Or maybe it's a habit of comparing Hermann to somebody else. Jason Abbot, for instance."

George walked back to the couch and sat down. "Alongside Abbot, Mister Hermann is a saint." He swallowed. "Rod, I've worked for the Hermann Land and Cattle Company for nine years. In that time I have never known it to rob a man or deal unfairly with its neighbors."

"That's a little hard to swallow."

"I've got to make you believe it, because I sent for you to offer you a job. Mister Hermann needs you, although he doesn't know it."

"The hell!" Rod leaned forward in the leather chair. "You know I'll be putting up hay in a week, but you fetch me here to offer me a job."

"So I'm a knuckle-headed idiot. But I had to try, Rod. I'd like us to be on the same side."

Rod sank back against the leather. "Go ahead. Maybe I'll let that hay go."

A slow grin broke across George's face. "I didn't think I'd hear that from you." He took the cigar out of his pocket. "Mister Hermann and Grace will be here tomorrow. They leave Gouge Eye early in the morning and I want you to meet them on the pass about noon. I'm hiring your gun, Rod. It's a job I wouldn't offer to any other man."

"You could meet him yourself," Rod said. "Why, hell, you've got a dozen men you could round up."

"I don't want to start the ball, Rod. That's just what I'd do if I showed my face in Poplar City."

"Take your crew . . ."

"I said I didn't want to start it. Anyhow, my boys are scattered from here to the Steens and out in the desert. I haven't got time, and Mister Hermann would raise hell if I did. He thinks a buckaroo's job is to look after cattle."

"What makes you think I can do the job?"

"I don't think, Rod, I know. I've followed everything you did from the day Dad died. I'd like to be the kind of man you are, but I never had it in me."

Rod rolled a smoke, his eyes on the brown paper that he twisted and sealed. He fished a match from his vest pocket and lighted the cigarette, taking his time. He could not believe he'd heard the words George had just said, George who had always been so sure of himself.

"Speaking of things you never thought you'd hear," Rod said finally, "that's something I never thought I'd hear."

George gave him a wry grin. "I wouldn't say it if I didn't need your help. Right now pride isn't important. The valley men are your friends. With you riding beside Mister Hermann and Grace, they won't have any trouble."

"I ain't your man," Rod said. "I don't have a friend in the valley except Frank Benson."

"I can't believe that . . ."

"I told you I had a fight with Sam Kane."

"You're still my man," George said stubbornly.

"You'll get Mister Hermann to Spade without any trouble. I want you to stay here till he leaves, and I don't have any idea when that'll be."

Rod rose. "I've got a spread to run. Ain't much, but it's all I've got."

"Name your figure."

"Might take all summer."

George nodded. "It might."

"Two thousand dollars. I'll stay here till he leaves the valley."

Rod had been sure that would end it, but without the slightest hesitation, George said: "I'll get it for you."

George left the room, returning presently with a bulging money belt that he handed to Rod. "This is the easiest way for you to carry it. Better count it."

"I'll take your word for it."

"Why did you want two thousand dollars?"

"That's what it takes to get Abbot off my neck."

George accepted that, not asking for an explanation. He glanced at his watch. "I'll go tell Wang to put another plate on the table." He started toward the dining room, then turned back. "Rod, I think you'll wind up liking Mister Hermann."

"You mean you're hoping."

"Maybe. I like him and I respect him, or I wouldn't have stayed with him for nine years. He's got more guts than any man I know. One time I saw him go up to a man who held a gun on him and take the gun away from the fellow. For anybody else it would have been stupid, but not for Mister Hermann."

George left the living room then. Rod moved to the door and stood looking at the blue, placid water of Egan Lake, but he wasn't actually seeing it. He was thinking of the expression he would see on Jason Abbot's face when he gave the horse trader the money.

The sun was barely showing above the eastern hills when Rod had breakfast in the hotel dining room the next morning. Neither Marcia nor Doll were up. Ada Larkin, Otto Larkin's oldest girl, who did most of the cooking for Marcia, brought Rod's order to him and returned at once to the kitchen. She was a tall bony woman who found it hard to smile. Rod thought now how seldom he had heard laughter except from Frank Benson and Doll during the three years he had lived here.

When he had finished eating, he left half a dollar on the table and went out into the cool, fresh morning. Later the day would be hot, but at this hour the night chill still clung to the air. It was one of the things Rod liked about this country, and was at least partly responsible for the absence of disease among the cattle.

Rod saddled his sorrel, thinking that he had

ample time to reach the pass before noon. He rode down the street and reined up in front of Abbot's office, not sure the man was up. He'd get Abbot out of bed if he was still sleeping, for he wanted to free his mind of the worry that owing money to Abbot had aroused in him.

He stepped down and racked his horse, hearing a rooster crow from a chicken pen on a side street. Someone was chopping wood, the sound of axe on pine carrying sharply to him through the thin, chill air. As Rod stepped up on the walk, the swamper came out of the Palace and slung a bucket of dirty water into the street, nodding a greeting.

He asked: "How do you feel this morning?"

"A little sore," Rod answered.

The swamper laughed. "Reckon Kane is too," he said, and went back into the saloon.

Rod swung around the hitch pole and tried the door of Abbot's office. It was locked. Rod knocked, and when there was no answer, he hammered on the door, wondering if Abbot had spent the night on his ranch with England and Webb. Then the lock clicked, the door swung open, and Abbot stood staring at Rod. His hair was disheveled and he was wearing only his pants and underclothes, and he seemed to be still drugged from sleep.

"Find my note," Rod said. "I'm paying you off."

Abbot, thoroughly awake, said: "Go to hell." He started to shut the door.

Rod got his boot over the threshold in time to keep Abbot from closing the door.

"What's the matter with you?" he asked. "I've got the money."

"Pay up when the note's due," Abbot said sullenly, still trying to shut the door.

Rod put a shoulder to the door. He drove against it and slammed it open, knocking Abbot halfway across the room. Rod went inside, staring at the horse trader.

He said: "You sure wanted your money the other night. What's hit you?"

Abbot scraped the tip of his fingers across his pointed chin, making a sandpapery sound in the silence, then he whirled and lunged toward his desk. He had a drawer open and was bringing a gun up when Rod reached him. He hit Abbot on the chin, slamming him back from the desk and half turning him around. Abbot fell against the wall, his feet sliding out from under him, and he sat down hard, his gun dropping from his hand.

Rod grabbed the gun and stepped back. "You out of your head, Jason?"

"Yeah, maybe I am." Abbot got up, pulled his swivel chair back from the desk, and sat down. "Devers, I've learned something. This country is too small for both of us."

"I've had that notion too." Rod placed Abbot's

gun on the desk. "Get your gun belt, Jason, and come into the street. We'll fix it so we won't be crowding each other."

"I'm not that big a fool," Abbot said thickly. "There are other ways."

"Like a shot in the back, maybe? All right, we'll wait, but right now you can get that note out and mark it paid. I've got the money."

"Where'd you get it?"

"My business."

"The only place you could get it would be Spade. Looks like you've gone over to Hermann like Sam said you had."

"I'm going to meet him this morning, which ain't no never mind to you. Now do you want your money or not?"

Abbot gave him a crafty look. "I figure the interest is forty dollars. Got that, too?"

"You said you'd overlook the interest . . ."

"You didn't take me up on that deal," Abbot said. "Go back to Spade for another forty dollars."

A feeling of defeat crept into Rod's belly again. His pride would not permit him to ask George for more money.

"You're playing a damned funny game, Jason. I've had my spring mudded up and my fences knocked down and a haystack burned. It won't work. I'm sticking to the Rocking R, but I'm mighty damned curious about why you want it."

"I don't. I just want you out of the country. You don't fit here. Move on."

"How do you figure?"

Abbot motioned to the door. "I'm busy. Vamoose."

Rod didn't move for a moment. He just stood staring down at Abbot and hating him as he had never hated before. He thought of Marcia and pitied her.

Finally he said: "Before we're done, I'll kill you. I reckon you're the one who had better get out of the country."

He wheeled out of the office, mounted, and left town at a gallop.

When he had gone a mile or so, he glanced back and saw that a rider was leaving Poplar City, headed north toward Sam Kane's SK—Abbot or some rider he had hired to go after Kane. The thought struck Rod that he had been foolish to tell Abbot about Hermann coming today, but then he decided it didn't make any difference. Whatever Abbot planned to do might just as well happen sooner than later.

The country began tilting upward and Rod climbed steadily, the rocky eastern rim of the valley covered by rabbit brush and a few stunted junipers. It was poor graze that no one claimed, although the day might come when it would be used, and then Rod remembered Sam Kane saying that Egan Valley was about the last place where a man could bring a few head of cows and get a start. Now only hardscrabble range was left, and it probably explained the position Sam Kane and the others had taken.

Near noon Rod reached the summit and reined up. He sat his saddle, studying the narrow, crooked road that looped back and forth on the eastern slope below and then faded away into a maze of cañons ten miles away. Rod had a bad moment, thinking that George had been mistaken about the day of Hermann's arrival, or that something bad had happened to him and his daughter.

Presently a buckboard appeared around a bend below him, and Rod grinned a little, wondering why he had become anxious about the welfare of a man he had hated for nine years. But that was the strangest part of the whole business. This thing had become so twisted that he was beginning to look upon Karl Hermann as an ally rather than an enemy.

Dismounting, Rod tied his sorrel to the lone juniper that grew on the wind-swept summit. He sat down on a rock beside the road and rolled a smoke.

Rod was still there when Hermann's buckboard wheeled up the last sharp pitch to the summit and stopped, Hermann eyeing Rod speculatively.

Rod rose and walked to the rig, his hand

extended. He said: "I'm Rod Devers, George's brother. George sent me here to fetch you to Spade."

"George's brother," Hermann said with an honest warmth. "I've heard of you, Devers. Heard a lot of you. Glad to know you."

Hermann gave Rod's hand a quick grip and then wrapped the lines around the whipstock. He stepped out of the buckboard, stretching, sharp eyes on Rod as he motioned to the girl in the seat.

"My daughter Grace, Devers. Probably George mentioned she'd be with me."

Rod nodded and touched the brim of his Stetson.

The girl was wearing a linen duster and a floppy-brimmed hat that was tied to her head by a scarf. The wind tugged at it, and she raised a hand as if afraid the scarf wouldn't hold. Rod could tell little about her looks because the combination of hat brim, scarf, and upturned duster collar almost masked her face.

"How do you do, Mister Devers," the girl said. "I hate wind. Does it always blow in this country?"

"Not so much in the valley." He turned to Hermann, who was standing beside the front wheel, his eyes on the valley below him. "You'll have trouble in Poplar City. Do you want to swing around the town?"

Hermann stood motionless, as if he hadn't

heard. He was the strangest looking cowman Rod had ever seen. He was in his middle fifties, short and pot-bellied round, with a rosy face that seemed a little comical under his black derby hat. He was wearing a brown broadcloth suit and button shoes, and if Rod had not known who he was, he would have mistaken the man for a drummer. There was nothing about him, not even the team of bays or the ancient buckboard, that resembled a hundred million dollars.

"Quite a sight," Hermann breathed in awe. "I'd heard about Egan Valley a long time before I bought Spade, but it's taken me all this time to get here. Mighty pretty, ain't it, Grace?"

"Yes, Daddy, but did you hear Mister Devers's question?"

"Question?" Hermann swung to face Rod. "I'm sorry. What did you ask me?"

"You'll have trouble in Poplar City. Do you want to swing around the town?"

Hermann smiled, his blue eyes twinkling. "We will not only go through the town, but we will eat dinner there. We had breakfast before sunup."

"Do you have a gun?"

"I never carry a gun." Hermann was suddenly grave. "Trouble's your business, ain't it?"

"No," Rod answered. "Not any more. I'm a cowman, Hermann. I own one critter to your ten thousand, but we're both cowmen. Trouble ain't my business any more than it's yours."

The girl laughed. "Well said, Mister Devers. For years I've been looking for a man who wasn't scared of Daddy. At last I've found one."

Hermann's eyes were twinkling again. "She's always looking for men, Devers, of one kind or another. She collects them, you know." He scratched his fat nose. "You're on Spade's payroll?"

"That's right."

"Then why ain't you taking care of my cattle instead of riding up here to meet us?"

"I was hired to meet you and ride to Spade with you. I suppose you could say that trouble is my business as long as you're in this country, but I took the job for just one reason. I needed money."

Hermann shook his head. "I don't understand George. He knows how I feel about things like this." He shoved his hands into his pockets and rocked back and forth on his feet. "As I remember it, you did not agree with George about going to work for me. Seems like you got your neck bowed about my bank taking over your dad's place. Happened nine years ago, I believe."

"You've got a good memory." Rod shrugged. "I still don't agree with George. He wanted a job with a big outfit. I wanted my own outfit. When you boil it all down, I reckon that's the real difference between me and George."

Hermann nodded. "I suppose it is. Well, I ain't one to say which of you is wrong. George has been loyal to me." He glanced at the gun on Rod's hip. "But I have an order against my men carrying firearms. Take yours off and throw it into the buckboard."

"Your orders don't apply to me," Rod said. "Maybe you'll savvy what I mean when we get to Poplar City."

Turning on his heel, Rod walked to his horse. He mounted and rode back.

Hermann was in the seat again, the lines in his hands. He said stiffly: "I won't have a man working for me who won't take my orders. You're fired."

"Daddy," the girl cried. "You don't know . . ."

"I have certain principles," Hermann said. "I never deviate from them."

"Your principles make money," Rod said, "which doesn't mean you know anything about the folks in Egan Valley."

"You're being stubborn, Daddy," Grace said hotly. "Talk to George before you fire this man."

"All right, I'll talk to George," Hermann agreed reluctantly, "but if you expect to stay on Spade's payroll, you'll do what I tell you."

Hermann spoke to his team and drove down the grade, Rod riding behind the rig.

George had said Karl Hermann had more guts than any other man he had ever known. Rod could now believe that. There was nothing amazing about Hermann's appearance. The girl

157

had called it right. Hermann was just stubborn. If he expected to impress Kane and Larkin and the others, he was mistaken.

They reached the valley floor, and Rod, touching his sorrel up, rode around the rig and took the lead. He had no idea what Kane and the others would do, but they'd be in town, waiting, probably a little drunk and certainly filled with Abbot's poison.

When Rod reached the edge of town, he saw the line of horses racked in front of the saloon. He reined around and turned in beside the buckboard.

"Your trouble's waiting for you," he told Hermann. "Let me do the talking."

Irritated, Hermann said: "I never have trouble. One of my principles is to get along with my neighbors."

"These boys don't aim to get along with you," Rod said.

Kane and the others had come out of the Palace, and now they moved into the street to form a solid line of sullen, dark-faced men, armed with rifles and six-guns. Rod ignored them and, reining in before the hotel, stepped down and tied his sorrel. Hermann pulled to the hitch rail and wrapped the lines around the whipstock.

"I take it you boys are my neighbors," Hermann said pleasantly. "I want to get acquainted with you before I leave town."

Rod moved to stand beside the buckboard. He said: "Take your daughter inside and order dinner. I'll be in after a while."

"I want to talk to these men," Hermann said truculently.

Kane leaned forward and spit into the dust. He wiped his mouth with the back of his hand, his face still raw and bruised from the beating Rod had given him. He said something in a low tone to Larkin and Larkin nodded. Then the line moved forward, both ends swinging toward the buckboard forming a semi-circle in the street.

"That's close enough." Rod's right hand dropped to his gun butt. "I'll kill the first man who comes any closer."

Jason Abbot was nowhere in sight, a fact which did not surprise Rod. Abbot was the author and producer of this drama, but he was not an actor. Probably he was watching from his office window, and he would remain there unless Rod rooted him out, something which he could not do now.

Barney Webb and Chuck England stood in front of the batwings of the Palace, their cold eyes on Rod. He had no idea what Abbot's orders had been, but it seemed a fair guess that the horse trader was depending on Kane and Larkin to do this job, that he would not want his men to have any part in it. If that was true, there was a chance bloodshed could be avoided, for Kane, even sullenly angry as he was now, had no desire to walk into a slug from Rod's gun.

For a moment there was no movement, no sound but the thin whine of the wind as it played against the eaves of the buildings facing Main Street. Rod's nerves tightened until he thought he could not stand here like this, but he could not force the issue as long as Hermann and Grace were in the buckboard.

Unexpectedly, Grace broke the tension.

"We'll go inside, Mister Devers," she said. "Come on, Daddy."

Rod still did not move until Grace and her father had stepped down from the buckboard. Hermann, standing on the boardwalk, said: "I would like to talk to these men in the hotel, Devers. If they have a grievance against Spade, or against George, I want to know what it is."

Kane stiffened.

Rod said sharply: "Stand pat, Sam."

A single hot word, a threatening motion would set this thing off. If it broke, Rod knew he would die—but Sam Kane would die, too, and it must have been that sobering knowledge which held Sam motionless. Rod heard the Hermanns cross the walk, followed by the lobby door being slammed shut by the wind.

"If it's talk you want, Sam," Rod said, "you and Larkin come into the lobby. The rest of you stay here."

160

But it was not talk that Kane wanted. He wheeled and stalked back toward the Palace. The rest looked at him and then at Rod. Larkin swore and swung sharply to follow Kane. The others disbanded. Rod waited until Webb and England went inside, knowing that nothing had been settled. Twice Sam Kane had reached for the mantle of leadership, and twice he had failed to wrap it around him. If his bruised pride outweighed his caution, the third time would be different.

Rod smiled wryly as he tied Hermann's team and went into the lobby. If Jason Abbot had been watching, he had seen an old truth demonstrated: if a man wanted a job done, he had better do it himself. That's exactly what he might do when the Hermanns left town.

No one was behind the desk. Rod turned into the dining room, hoping to see Doll, but neither she nor her mother was in sight. Ada Larkin stood at the table where the Hermanns were seated, her plain, angular face expressionless.

"Steak," Rod said as he sat down, and when Ada turned and walked toward the kitchen, Rod nodded at Grace Hermann. "Thanks for getting your dad out of the buckboard. You've got more sense than he has."

Grace had taken off her linen duster and hat. She was wearing a black suit, and now that Rod had a close look at her without anything hiding part of her face, he saw that she was a fine-looking woman, a little older than he had first guessed, and fully matured. Her wide mouth curved easily into a smile. Her blue eyes were twinkling as she looked at Rod.

"Daddy hates to admit that, Mister Devers," she said, "but I agree with you. I'm smarter than he is."

Hermann scowled. "Stop your bragging . . . I'm smart enough." He looked at Rod. "What's wrong here, Devers?"

"They're afraid of you," Rod answered. "It's that simple. They think you're going to grab the whole valley. So being that's the way they see it, the easiest way to protect themselves is to put you out of the way."

"I don't want the damned valley," Hermann said hoarsely. "I'm going to tell them . . ."

"You think they'd listen?" Rod demanded. "Or if they did, do you think they'd believe you?" He shook his head. "Look, Hermann. Little men are afraid of big men. You must have been up against it before."

"I've always been able to talk to men," Hermann said. "Go fetch the leaders over here. I can make them believe me."

"Won't do you no good to get me killed," Rod said. "My job is to get you to Spade alive. Maybe you don't care about your own hide, but you've got your daughter to think about."

Grace smiled at her father. "That's right," she commented.

"But I don't savvy," Hermann said. "They don't have any grounds for their suspicion. I want to tell them the truth."

"What you tell 'em won't prove anything," Rod said impatiently. "If you can figure out a way to show 'em you want to be a good neighbor, you can prove your intentions . . . but they won't believe anything you say if you talk for a week."

"The people in this valley don't know me," Hermann said bitterly. "I want them to, Devers. And I want to know them."

Rod leaned back in his chair, impatience at Hermann's stubbornness growing in him. He could not tell the cattleman what Marcia had said about Abbot, and apparently Hermann did not realize that his reputation had grown until he had become a sort of terrifying legend to the valley settlers.

"Do one thing," Rod said after a moment's silence. "Don't jump the traces until I get you to Spade. Talk to George."

"But you know . . . ," Hermann began.

"Daddy," Grace interrupted, "you do what Mister Devers says. It's George's job to tell you, not his."

Glowering, Hermann shifted his weight in his chair and reached for a cigar. Ada Larkin came out of the kitchen, her heels tapping sharply on the floor. Rod thought she was bringing their dinner, but when he looked up, he saw that her hands were empty.

Bending over him so that her mouth was close to his ear, she whispered: "Missus Nance wants to see you in her parlor." She whirled and walked rapidly back to the kitchen.

Rod hesitated, glancing at Hermann, then he rose. "Excuse me," he said, and left the dining room.

He walked down the hall to Marcia's parlor, feeling a little uneasy. At this time of day Marcia was usually behind the desk, and Doll always waited on tables through the dinner hour. He wondered if there was some reason for their not wanting Hermann to see them. The door to Marcia's parlor was open, and he went in.

Marcia was sitting in her rocking chair and Doll was standing by the window. Both were pale and plainly nervous.

The uneasiness grew in Rod. What had happened in the street was no concern of theirs.

"Sit down," Marcia said.

"I haven't got time," Rod said. "I left the Hermanns waiting at a table."

"I know," Marcia said. "It won't hurt them to wait."

"Not unless the Hermann woman finds it hard to do without your company," Doll breathed. "I know now why you don't want to marry me."

He stared at her, not understanding. She was glaring at him, her temper edgy, and he could see no hint of the bouncy, gay humor which ordinarily dominated her. Because his own nerves were taut, he said more sharply than he intended to: "You should. I've told you enough times."

"You haven't told me the truth," Doll snapped. "You're looking for bigger game."

He understood then. Hot words were on his lips. He checked them, sensing that both Doll and Marcia were under some strain he didn't understand.

"Did you fetch me back here to talk about that, Marcia?" Rod asked.

She shook her head. "Doll's imagination is running wild." She lowered her eyes to her hands that were clasped on her lap. "Rod, I wouldn't say this if I wasn't convinced you were in love with Doll. I don't want you killed for that reason, but you can't blame Doll for thinking what she does. If you do love her, you'll save your life . . . for her."

He leaned against the door jamb, looking at Marcia and then at Doll. "I don't know what a man needs to do to prove he's in love with a woman." He brought his gaze back to Marcia. "I took the job George gave me because it's the one way I can get Jason Abbot off my neck. I've got to finish the job. I've already been paid."

"You don't have to finish the job," Marcia

cried. "The main thing you've got to do is to keep on living. If you go back into the street, Barney Webb will kill you. Let the Hermanns go on by themselves, Rod."

He was certain now that there was something here he didn't understand, something they wouldn't tell him. The thought struck him that Marcia had a stake in Abbot's game, that the things she had said when he'd had his fight with Kane had been lies, or, at best, only part of the truth.

He said stubbornly: "I made a deal with George. I'll keep my part of the deal."

He wheeled and walked back down the hall. He heard Doll cry out: "Rod, Rod!" But he kept on and, crossing the lobby, went into the dining room and sat down.

Ada had brought the Hermanns their dinner. Now she came out of the kitchen with his steak and coffee, and walked away, her face still barren of expression.

They ate in silence, Hermann sullen and Grace appearing to enjoy the excitement of the moment. When they had finished the meal, Hermann rose.

"Let's get moving, Devers," he said shortly.

"No hurry," Rod said, glancing out of the window. The street was empty, but if Barney Webb were waiting for him, he'd show up the instant Rod appeared.

Hermann stopped by the lobby door and took

his derby hat off the rack. He said: "I'm in a hurry."

"You're following orders," Grace said sharply. "Remember?"

Hermann put his derby on his head, saying nothing. Ada came out of the kitchen and he paid her for their meals. Grace slipped into her duster and tied her hat on her head with her scarf.

She asked: "You think there will be more trouble?"

"Yes. Stay inside the lobby till I tell you to come out." Rod drew his gun from its holster and replaced it; he glanced at Hermann's stormy face. "We have no law here, which is something you'll have to get used to. We're too far from the county seat for the sheriff to bother with us."

"I'll change that," Hermann said harshly. "I'm paying enough taxes to deserve some protection."

"You're getting protection," Rod said, and went out into the sunshine.

The street was still empty, but he saw at once that Marcia had been right.

Barney Webb came out of the Palace. He called: "Devers!"

Rod moved along the boardwalk until he reached the end of the hitch pole. For three years he had been a rancher, slow years, without violence. It was the life he wanted. All the time he had been earning gunfighter's wages, his mind had reached ahead to the day when he could hang up his gun. Now he was back to where he had been, and the strangest part of it was that he was fighting for Karl Hermann.

The old poison of hatred was gone. Hermann was not a man who was easy to hate. Rod had been wrong and George had been right, except for one thing. He admired Hermann to the point where he exaggerated the man's power and courage. Up here Hermann's wealth and power could not save him. Only Rod's gun could do that.

Rod didn't say anything to Webb. Words would be wasted. Webb had stepped down off the walk, his pale blue eyes cold. He stood waiting, tense, expectant.

In this strange, drawn-out moment the silence seemed to symbolize the three years Rod had spent on the Rocking R. Now it was as if these years had never been. Time had made the complete turn.

In the sharp afternoon sunlight Rod saw Barney Webb's face clearly, a thin, tight-featured face that needed a shave, the calculating blue eyes like those of so many gunmen Rod had known. Suddenly fear touched Rod as he wondered if the three years had slowed his draw, but then the fear was gone. He could not afford it. He had to kill. He had too much to live for to let Webb kill him.

Rod took a slow step forward, his right hand

hovering near the butt of his gun. Webb had never seen Rod pull a gun. Uncertain of his superiority, he had let this play out, hoping that Rod would break, that in a crazy burst of panic he would go for his gun and throw a wild shot. But Rod had never given way to panic, and he didn't now. He took one more step and it was Webb who broke under the pressure, his right hand sweeping down toward his gun.

Two shots hammered out, drowning out the silence. Powder flame danced from gun muzzles and died. It was close, Webb's bullet slicing through Rod's vest under his left armpit. A few inches to the right and Rod would have been a dead man.

Webb was partly turned by Rod's bullet. His knees gave under him and he fell, his hat coming off his bald head as he went down. He rolled over on his left side, lips tightly drawn against his teeth. He had dropped his gun. Now he gripped it again and tilted it. Once more Rod fired and Webb's face dropped down into the dust.

Rod did not move. He held his smoking gun, eyes on the batwings of the saloon. He wondered where Chuck England was, where Jason Abbot was. He was not sure what Kane and his friends would do. Then the batwings were flung open, and Kane came out, Larkin and the others behind him.

"You boys taking this up?" Rod called.

Kane stood over Webb's body, hating Rod and fearing him, but sobered by what had happened.

He said: "Not today. Get out of the country, Devers."

"Where's England and Abbot?"

Kane did not answer. He knelt beside Webb's body and felt the man's wrist, and then he rose. He was not man enough for the job he himself had given, and he plainly showed that he felt the overpowering weight of his own futility.

He shouted in a high, crazy voice: "Get out of town, Devers! Take the Hermanns with you!" Later Kane would regret what he had done, but at the moment, standing beside Webb's body, he was incapable of taking a stand.

Hermann and Grace came out of the hotel. They got into the buckboard and drove down the street. Quickly Rod untied his sorrel and stepped up into the saddle, his gun still in his hand. The stunning impact of death held Kane and his bunch motionless, but it might not last. Rod dug steel into the flanks of his sorrel. He caught up with the Hermanns at the edge of town before he holstered his gun.

"What kind of a damned wild country is this?" Hermann shouted.

"You should have looked into it when you bought Spade," Rod said. "Ask George."

Grace looked at him, her face still flushed with excitement. "You're a brave man."

"Not brave," he said impatiently. "A man does only what he has to do. In my book that ain't bravery."

They were silent then, Rod riding beside the buckboard. He was a little weak now that it was over, and sick with the knowledge that this was only the beginning. One death led to another, once the first blood had been shed. That was the pattern that had begun to take shape, and no man could tell where it would stop.

For a time Rod was so lost in his thoughts that he ignored the Hermanns. A question kept nagging his mind until he was nearly driven frantic by the elusive answer. Where had Chuck England been during the fight with Barney Webb?

Rod didn't waste any time wondering about Jason Abbot. The horse trader had probably been in his office watching the fight. He was not one to take chips in a fracas when he had two hired gun hands to take the risks, but Abbot would certainly have done everything he could to make sure that Rod was killed. Sam Kane and Otto Larkin had proved they were unequal to the task, so it had come back to Abbot's men. But why had Barney Webb been given the job while England remained out of sight?

Rod had the feeling that Webb had been very sure of himself when he had stepped out of the Palace. A minute, perhaps, had passed before

Webb had pulled his gun. Now, recalling the expression on Barney Webb's face and the way he had played for time, it seemed to Rod that he had become less sure of himself as those seconds passed.

Was it possible that England was supposed to come into the play and something had held him out?

Rod shook his head, exasperated. He could not think of anything that would have kept England out of the fight. It was inconceivable that the man would have remained inside the Palace after Webb was down and Kane and his bunch had come into the street.

They had swung west along the north shore of the lake, and now they reached the sand reef and Hermann pulled up. Rod, jerked out of his thoughts, became aware that they had almost reached Spade and that Hermann was leaning forward in his seat, his eyes on the lake.

Grace gave Rod a tolerant smile. "He's hypnotized himself, Mister Devers. We are about to see a new thought being born."

Rod reined up in the grass beside the buckboard. He nodded and was silent, not having the slightest idea what was in Hermann's mind. But something was churning there, and it occurred to Rod that Hermann was both a dreamer and a practical man, a rare combination that perhaps accounted for the fabulous success he had made.

Some sandhill cranes were engaged in a crazy, flapping dance. Slender avocets gave out their melancholy cry. Curlews, long-billed and nosey, talked in their "cur-lee" language. A belligerent Canada goose honked a challenge and was immediately set upon by a trumpeter swan and soundly beaten. Then the swan came up on the shore, arching his wings and strutting as if he had accomplished a great thing.

Grace laughed and glanced at Rod again. "A three-ring circus," she said, and Rod nodded.

Hermann apparently had not seen the show. "Looks like a lot of shallow water along the shore," he said. "If that sand reef went out, there would be a sizable piece of lake bottom exposed. It would be a chore to drain it and get rid of the tules, but it could be done."

Rod nodded again, still silent. An observing man, Karl Hermann. In these few minutes he had hit upon the same idea that everyone in the valley had talked about, but apparently the question of ownership had not occurred to him. Rod didn't feel called upon to mention it. The sand reef had been here a long time and it would probably continue to be here, but if Hermann took it on himself to blast a channel in the reef, he'd find himself with more trouble on his hands than he had now.

Hermann swung a hand in a wide circle away

from the lake. "Looks like it's all George said it was, Devers, but I'm wondering about something. Is the valley land ever flooded?"

"It is along the streams," Rod answered. "That's why you always have the grass."

"And hay," Hermann said thoughtfully. "But if we had this marginal land drained, we could raise hay here and we'd have more grazing land. Isn't that right?"

"Sure," Rod said, "but I suppose you've got a million acres of mountain and desert graze. The bunchgrass that's native to this country is the best there is. You don't need any more."

"Not for the size herd I have now," Hermann agreed, "but I didn't make my money by being satisfied with what I had. I'll see what George says."

Hermann spoke to the team then, and the buckboard wheeled on across the dike, Rod riding behind the rig. A few minutes later they crossed the bridge that spanned Halfmile Creek and went up the sharp slope to Spade's yard.

George came out of the big ranch house, calling a greeting. Grace waved to him, but Hermann sat motionless.

"Welcome to Spade," George said genially as he came to the buckboard.

"It's beautiful," Grace said. "The best ranch we own. You didn't exaggerate it a bit."

George held up a hand and helped Grace down.

He put his arms around her and kissed her. Rod, surprised at this greeting, thought there was little ardor in the way Grace returned his kiss. She stepped back from him and turned to her father.

"You're looking at an ungrateful man, George," Grace said.

Hermann wrapped the lines around the whip-stock and, stepping down, offered his hand. "I've seen some things today I don't like, George."

If George was bothered by Hermann's attitude, he gave no sign as he shook his employer's hand.

"I know, Mister Hermann. I know exactly what you're thinking, but you're here safe and sound. I was worried."

"You had cause to be," Rod said drily.

"George, you know . . ." Hermann began.

"Stop it, Daddy," Grace interrupted angrily. "If it hadn't been for Rod, we wouldn't be here, and I doubt that you'd be alive."

George pinned his eyes on Rod. "Trouble?"

"Plenty," Rod said. "Kane and his bunch were waiting in town for us. When we left the hotel after dinner, Barney Webb jumped me. I killed him." He motioned toward Hermann. "I don't know how much your boss values his hide, but he's an ungrateful cuss, for a fact."

Hermann drew his shoulders back, his face suddenly red. "Damn it, this is not a proposition of being grateful. George, I don't know what the trouble is, but you've let it get out of hand. That's what I don't like."

"Come in and I'll tell you what's been happening," George said, still maintaining his composure. "Juan, take care of the horses. Mister Hermann, this is Juan Herrera. He was with Clay Cummings when Clay drove his first herd into the valley."

Juan had come out of the barn. He bowed and grinned. "*Saludos, mi patron*," he said.

The frostiness thawed from Hermann at once. He walked toward Herrera and held out his hand. "I remember Clay's speaking about you, Juan. I'm glad to know you."

Pleased, the old man bobbed his head.

Rod, watching, felt an increased respect for Karl Hermann. Out of the thousands of men who worked for him, he remembered his agreement with Clay Cummings about Juan Herrera. Another reason for his success, Rod thought. A man in Hermann's position had to have loyalty, and this touch of kindliness was probably typical of him and accounted for the loyalty which a smaller man would never have attained.

Hermann turned with Grace and George toward the house.

Rod said: "I'll take care of my horse."

"Come in as soon as you can," George said. "Supper is almost ready."

Rod took his time, not knowing what would be

expected of him now, and preferring to stay in the bunkhouse. He smoked a cigarette, loitering for a few minutes in the shade of a poplar, the sun well over toward the west. He thought of Doll and Marcia, wondering how Marcia had known what Barney Webb would do. There could be only one answer. Abbot had told her his plan. That reminded him of the other question that had been bothering him. What about Chuck England?

Resentment touched him when he thought of Doll, and her insinuation that he had put off their marriage in the hope of making a better one with Grace. He was used to her violent and willful moods, but he had never known her to be jealous. Well, she had made herself plain enough. He could not hope that their relationship would ever be the same. Perhaps it was his fault, tying together as he had his ambition to own a ranch and his love for Doll.

She had said she wouldn't come second to a ranch—she had to be first or nothing. She hadn't understood, she hadn't even tried. If he could have lived these last few days over, he would have made the same choice. She was selfish, he thought bitterly. She wanted her own way just for the sake of having it. So he had lost her. But perhaps it was just as well.

He flipped his cigarette stub away and went on to the house. No one was in the living room, but he heard George and Hermann talking in the office. Rod went back to the porch and sat down, his back against a post.

He heard heels click on the porch and, turning his head, saw that Grace was coming toward him. She had put on a black velvet dress, cut a little too low, he thought, and a little too tight around the hips, an expensive dress that did exactly what she wanted it to do for her. It was quite plain except for a lace ruffle around her throat and a row of white buttons down the front. She wore a pearl necklace that probably represented a small fortune.

As he rose she asked: "Like it?"

"Sure. Looks about like ten thousand dollars."

She smiled. "Not quite. I'm wearing it for you."

"I thought it would be for George."

A small smile touched the corners of her mouth. "We'll let him think so."

She stopped, her head cocked.

Inside the office Hermann was shouting: "Damn it, George, what's got into you? Two thousand dollars for a few hours of a man's time. You keep saying that bunch of settlers would have killed me. That's loco. I wanted to talk to them, but your brother never gave me a chance."

Grace's face turned bitter. "Come inside, Rod. George needs help."

She whirled and went back into the house. Reluctantly Rod followed, thinking that this

178

side of Karl Hermann was exactly what he had expected.

"You'd better fire me," George said. "I did what I did because your safety seemed more important than any amount of money. You simply don't understand the feeling in the valley."

"Then it's your fault for letting it . . . ," Hermann stopped, aware that Grace stood in the doorway.

"You're being stubborn again, Daddy," she said coldly. "And downright foolish. I was with you, you know. It might have been different if you were alone."

"But George paid his brother two thousand dollars just . . ."

"Just to save our lives," she broke in. "Rod Devers has already earned it if he doesn't do another thing."

Hermann ran a hand through his hair, glaring at Grace, and then suddenly the anger flowed out of him. "You're right. Forget it, George."

"Am I fired?" George asked.

"Hell no. You're the last man in my organization I'd fire."

George wheeled and walked out. He said to Rod: "You'll want to wash up."

Rod said nothing while he followed George down the hall to the back porch. After he had washed, he found a comb and ran it through his hair.

Watching him, George said: "You've seen several sides of Mister Hermann today."

"Reckon I have."

"But he's not what you thought he was, is he? You don't hate him, do you?"

Rod's answer seemed important to George. Rod said: "No, I guess you were right about Dad losing his place. I don't think Hermann knew anything about it."

"I'm sure of it," George said.

They went back down the hall and into the dining room, where Hermann and Grace were already waiting. It was a quiet meal, a little too grand for Rod with the shiny silverware and the candlelight and the lace tablecloth. But it suited George, and Rod found himself wondering what George's relationship was with Grace. She had gone out of her way to tell Rod she was wearing the velvet dress for him and not George, but she didn't want to tell George. Well, it was their business, Rod thought. As soon as he finished up his part of the bargain, he'd be glad to get away from Spade.

When they returned to the living room, twilight was moving across the valley. George lighted the pink, hob-nailed lamp on the mahogany table in the middle of the big room and turned to Grace.

"I haven't changed anything in the house since Clay moved out," he said. "How do you like this room?"

She was sitting on the leather couch, slumped wearily, her legs stretched in front of her. She said: "It's an amazing room to find out here in the middle of nowhere, George, but the whole house and the ranch are amazing. I'd like to meet Clay Cummings."

"You will," George said. "Clay's in town, and he'll stop on his way back. He always spends a night here. I guess he likes to look things over. This house is still home to him, I suppose."

Hermann lighted a cigar and threw the match into the fireplace. He stood there, looking at George, and it struck Rod how much alike they were. In another twenty years George would resemble his employer even more than he did now.

"I want to see this country, George," Hermann said. "Really see it, because I'm convinced that what we have here is just a beginning. While we're riding around, your brother can look after Grace."

Grace smiled. "I was hoping it would work that way."

Rod's agreement with George did not include running herd on a girl, but before he could say so, a man called out: "Devers!"

It was a familiar voice, but for a moment Rod could not place it.

George wheeled toward the door, his face pale. "Excuse me," he said, and hurried from the room.

"Who's that?" Hermann asked.

"I don't know," Rod said, and moved to the door.

A man was standing beside the poplars in front of the house, the reins of his horse in his hand. Rod's breath was jolted out of him as suddenly as if he'd been struck in the stomach. It was Todd Shannon, the shifty-eyed, furtive Todd Shannon who belonged to Jason Abbot. Then Rod remembered what Sam Kane had said about George being behind the "accidents" that had been plaguing him. It couldn't be true, Rod thought, but what other reason would bring Shannon here?

III

Rod slept in the bunkhouse that night, or tried to sleep, but the hours dragged out while he lay staring at the black ceiling, his body rigid. Irritated by Juan Herrera's gurgling snores, he got up and sat for a time in the doorway and smoked a cigarette, hardly aware of the night sounds—the hooting of an owl, the mournful cry of a bird from the lake, the yapping of the coyotes on some distant rim.

George had given no explanation when he had returned from talking to Todd Shannon, and if he realized that Rod had recognized Shannon, he gave no indication of it. If George's visitor had been anyone but Todd Shannon! Rod thought about Marcia's saying that Jason Abbot wanted to murder Karl Hermann. Was it possible that George was somehow involved in Abbot's scheming, that Todd Shannon was a connecting link between George and Abbot?

Rod returned to his bunk, telling himself it wasn't possible, that George was not the kind of man who would be involved with Abbot, and that his loyalty to Hermann was beyond question. Still, sleep was elusive. No amount of self-assurance could blot out the suspicion that was in his mind; there was no logical explanation for

Shannon's visit except the one which Rod refused to accept.

Rod ate breakfast in the cook shack with Herrera and the blacksmith and Pablo Sanchez, who had ridden in late the evening before. Herrera harnessed Hermann's team and hooked it up, and George left with Sanchez and Hermann, still giving no explanation. Grace would want to take a ride later in the morning, George said, and he told Herrera to throw a side-saddle on the bay mare named Lady when Grace was ready.

She did not make her appearance until after ten. She came out of the house wearing a tan riding skirt and a broad-brimmed hat. She moved with a quick, easy grace, her hazel eyes bright with good humor. She was attractive and desirable, and very much a woman. Rod found himself liking her, even against his will. He had misjudged her even more than he had her father. He had supposed she was spoiled and willful and used to luxury, that she would complain and expect to be waited on hand and foot. Instead he found her good company. She was an expert rider, and she fell in love with Lady.

The first day set the pattern for the week, except that Sanchez returned to the cow camp. Hermann and George took the buckboard, or a two-wheeled cart when Hermann wanted to see the desert west of the valley. They were always gone until sundown, taking a lunch with them, and when they sat in the living room after supper, Hermann's good humor seemed to grow daily.

Once, in the middle of the week when they were alone, Rod asked George how long the Hermanns were staying.

"They haven't said," George answered.

"You hired me to look out for Hermann, but instead I'm turning out to be Grace's riding pardner."

"You'll have your chance to look out for Mister Hermann," George said somberly. "He's bound to see Kane and that whole damned bunch. He thinks he can straighten this trouble out." He paused, eyes pinned on Rod's face. "Can he?"

"Not as long as Jason Abbot is alive and Kane and his outfit trust him."

"That's what I figured." George scratched an ear, smiling a little. "You don't object to being Grace's riding pardner, do you?"

"No, but anybody could ride around with Grace."

George shook his head. "You're wrong on that. She's a hard woman to satisfy." He scratched his ear again, his face going sour. "I know better than anyone how hard she is to satisfy. She's falling in love with you, Rod, maybe on account of what happened in town the day they got here. You're lucky. Or maybe unlucky, depending on how you look at it."

George wheeled and walked away. Rod watched him, thinking that this was the damnedest thing he'd ever heard. He was no ladies' man, and Grace was about as likely to fall in love with him as a pig was to grow wings.

After that, he was often aware of her eyes on him, studying him, and she had a sort of proprietary attitude toward him. She insisted that he eat dinner with her in the house instead of the cook shack, and even when they had come in from their rides, he found it hard to get away from her. She lingered around the corrals or the barns just to be with him, and Herrera always seemed to disappear. Once, she came into the bunkhouse, for lack of anything better to do. He was sitting at the table playing solitaire.

"I know a woman isn't supposed to be out here," she said frankly, "but I don't see any sense in sitting in the house alone."

She lay down on a bunk, her head propped up on one hand. Rod went on playing, trying to pretend he was unaware of her shapely legs and the high mounds of her breasts, pressed tight against her blouse.

She wasn't like Doll, he thought, who, when the mood was upon her, would taunt him with light talk about how much he needed her and how cold the winter nights were when a man lived alone. Grace was more subtle. Without saying a word

186

she managed to let him know that all he had to do was to reach for her.

He would, he told himself, if it wasn't for Doll—and he always admitted to himself that made him the world's biggest fool. Doll had left no doubt in his mind that she was finished with him. If she believed he had given her up to make a try for Grace, he might as well do what she suspected of him. But he didn't, and now he wished uneasily that Grace would go back into the house where she belonged.

She laughed softly. "Put those cards down, Rod. After all, you don't often have a woman visitor in the bunkhouse."

"No." He laid a red queen on a black king. "You like to make it rough on a man."

She laughed again. "You've got that wrong, mister. You make it hard on a woman." She was silent, her face suddenly grave, then she said: "George tells me you have a little ranch in the foothills."

He nodded. "The Rocking R."

"I'd like to see it."

He looked up, startled. "I can't take you off Spade range, not with things the way they are."

"Things won't stay the way they are," she said. "I don't know what Daddy plans, but it'll work, whatever it is. It always does. He won't stand for trouble, even if it costs him a lot of money to avoid it."

187

There was nothing to say to that, so he went on playing. Money wouldn't touch Jason Abbot, and George ought to tell Hermann. But the chances were George wouldn't tell Hermann anything, not as long as he was being blamed for the trouble.

"You're not like George at all," Grace said. "He's very practical and a little dull. You're interesting, Rod. I suppose it's because you don't talk much."

He laid his cards down. "Nothing to talk about," he said.

"Yes there is. George says you want your own place. Isn't that kind of foolish when you could have a good job with us?"

"I reckon it is, the way you look at it," he said sharply, "but that's not my way. It's George's way."

She sat up and swung her feet to the floor. "You might change, Rod. Daddy needs a man like you. He knows it now, even if he didn't want to admit it the day we arrived." She rose and rubbed her back, smiling wryly. "I hope my saddle isn't as sore as I've been, but I'm getting tough. Tomorrow I'll have Wang fix a lunch. I want to ride into the mountains."

She went out. Rod didn't finish his game. There was no fun in it now. He rolled a smoke, tipping his chair back. Suddenly he felt an urge to saddle his sorrel and ride out. He wanted to see the

Rocking R again. Maybe the grass was right for cutting. He wanted to talk to Frank Benson and hear his big laugh; he wanted to see Doll again. Then the desire died in him. He didn't really want to see Doll. It was up to her now.

They left about nine the next morning, riding south across the grass, the lunch sack tied behind Rod's saddle. They reached a gap in the hills before noon and followed Bearclaw River for a mile, then stopped and ate lunch. Clouds were building up along the western horizon. Rod watched them uneasily, thinking that a storm was overdue.

"We'd better go back," he said.

She looked at him, surprised. "I'm going into the mountains. I've been looking at them every day we've been here, and now that we're this close I'm not going back."

"A storm's coming," he said.

"You're not sugar or salt," she jeered. "You won't melt." She turned to the river and stared down into a deep pool at the dark shadowy trout. "There's one down there a foot and a half long, Rod. We should have brought our fishing poles."

"No use of our getting wet," he said doggedly. "When we get a summer storm, it's likely to be a walloping good one."

"I'm not afraid of storms." She turned and put her hands on his arms, her face upturned, her red

189

lips slightly parted. "Rod, I want to meet Clay Cummings. You said he'd be along."

"He will," Rod said, puzzled. "What made you think of him?"

"Something George said the other evening. About Cummings building the house and furnishing it for his wife who couldn't stand to be alone, so she left him. I feel sorry for him. I mean, when a man does that much for a woman, she must be pretty small to just go off and leave him. I wouldn't . . . not if I loved him."

He turned away and walked toward the horses. Without knowing it, Grace had opened his old wound. He'd had all this week to think about Doll, and the more he'd thought, the less excuse he could see for her acting the way she had. He hadn't built a fine house as Cummings had, but he'd made a start, and it had been for Doll.

She was cheap and small, he thought savagely. He'd get the other forty dollars he needed, someway. He'd pay Abbot off and then he'd be where he wanted to be—alone. And next winter his bed would be just as cold as it had been for the past three winters.

He led the horses back to where Grace waited; he gave her a hand up into the saddle. He mounted, and they turned south along the willow-lined river. Clouds had rolled up into the sky, black and ominous, and the wind, coming in off the desert, smelled wet and tangy with sage.

"I was married once, Rod," Grace said. "Maybe you didn't know." He shook his head and she went on. "I thought maybe George had told you. He knew all about it. Well, it didn't work. I was young and pig-headed and I went against Daddy's advice in marrying the man."

She glanced at him, her face shadowed by unhappy memory. He was silent, not knowing quite what was expected of him. He wondered why George hadn't told him. It didn't make any difference to him, but perhaps it had to George.

"Daddy says I'm like a hot-blooded mare," she said ruefully. "I need someone who can hold a tight rein on me. You know . . . a strong man." She laughed shakily. "The trouble is you don't find many men like that. I could have had George. I still can, but it wouldn't do. I told him so the other night."

Rod glanced up at the sky that was black and forbidding. Lightning slashed across it and thunder made a wicked rumble.

"We've got to go back," he said.

She shivered as the wind struck at her. "It's too late, Rod. I've been stubborn and foolish, but it's no good now to say I'm sorry. George said there was a line cabin up here," Grace said uneasily. "Not far from a creek. He said there was grub and dry wood there."

"You know more about this country than I do,"

he said. "You didn't aim to find that line cabin, did you?"

She met his gaze blandly. "I just asked George in case something happened that we couldn't get back, and I guess it's happening. I wouldn't be afraid with you anyhow, Rod. You have a talent for shaping circumstances instead of letting circumstances shape you."

"You wouldn't be doing some shaping yourself, would you?"

"I might."

"Well, let's find that creek."

The rumble of thunder grew louder as they set out.

Rod touched the sorrel up, and within half a mile reached a small, white-maned stream that chattered noisily as it pounded toward the river.

"It's up there," Grace said. "I can see it."

The first drops of rain hit them then. "Come on!" Rod called, and swung up the creek. It would be touch and go, he thought, with the cabin a quarter of a mile away.

She kept up with him, horses laboring on the grade. Rod glanced back. A black curtain of rain was moving across the valley toward them. They wouldn't make it, he thought, and they didn't.

They were fifty yards from the cabin when it struck, hitting them with the violence of water thrown from a bucket. Within a few seconds they were soaked.

They pulled up in front of the cabin.

"Go inside!" Rod shouted above the racket of the storm. "I'll put the horses in the shed!"

She slid out of the saddle and ran into the cabin. Rod rode on to the shed, leading her mount. He took a moment to strip gear from the horses, then he went outside and shut the shed door and sprinted toward the cabin, head down. He went in, smelling the musty odor of a place that had not been lived in for months.

When he closed the door, the light in the room was very thin. Grace was standing in the middle of the room, hugging herself and shivering. There was a candle on the table. Rod found a can partly filled with matches.

"Light the candle," he said, and gave her a match.

Juniper wood was piled along the wall. Apparently it hadn't occurred to Grace to start a fire, he thought irritably. She hadn't even looked for matches. He got a fire going, and in a moment the crackle of it was a pleasant sound in the room. Grace remained by the table, watching him intently, the thin light of the candle on her face.

He looked at her, the irritation leaving him. She'd do. The average woman would be blaming him for her discomfort, but Grace was a long way from being average. Rod had started this job hating her father and believing he would dislike her. Now, in spite of himself, he admired Karl

Hermann. He didn't know how he felt about Grace, but he had been dead wrong about her.

Grace walked slowly over to him, put her hands on his arms, and tugged gently at him. "Rod," she said. "Rod."

He put his arms around her. Her face was upturned to his, and when he kissed her, she clung to him, making no secret of her hunger. Then she drew back, a hand caressing his cheek.

"I wouldn't make that ride back to Spade tonight for anything," she breathed. "You can't leave me alone, Rod."

He couldn't and he didn't want to. What a hell of a kink life had put in his twine. He had lost Doll and now he had Grace. But Grace wouldn't like the Rocking R. She wouldn't live there with him. It was a transient thought which left his mind at once, for it had nothing to do with this moment.

The afternoon was almost gone when Rod and Grace returned to Spade. The day had been warm and clear, and Grace had insisted on riding to the top of the mountains before they started back. Yesterday's storm had cleared away the haze which had blurred the buttes to the west; it had given the earth a clean-scented smell.

Grace, awed by the size and beauty of this country, had been silent while she sat her saddle, her eyes on the somber-hued desert that lay beyond the valley of the Bearclaw and ran on and on until it met the sky.

As they rode back to Spade, Rod thought about the way Grace had sat there so long, as if unable to fully satisfy the hunger that this country aroused in her.

It was another unexpected side of her character that surprised him. She didn't mention it on the way to the ranch, but he was convinced she wasn't pretending, that all the luxury and social position which money could buy had not fully compensated for a part of life which she had missed.

The thought that had briefly touched his mind the afternoon before was there again. Grace would not be willing to share his dream and his work and the inevitable hardships which were bound to go with the development of the Rocking R. Even if she lived at Spade, she would in time tire of the slow-paced and often dreary life of the cattle country.

Then a restlessness was in him, and he thought bitterly that he had lost the only really important thing in his life when he had lost Doll. No woman—Grace or any other—would ever take Doll's place.

He could not help comparing Doll and Grace. In many ways Doll was still immature, but in spite of her changeable and often violent moods, she had every characteristic that a wife should have. Maturity would come to her with the responsibility of marriage. But Grace was already a woman, pliant in some regards, doggedly stubborn in others. In the end the man she married would bow to her. It wouldn't do for Rod.

The Spade buildings were in sight when Grace said: "You're being mysterious again, Rod."

He stared straight ahead, remembering that he had perversely refused to tell her he loved her. He realized that when a man lost one woman, he instinctively turned to another, so he hadn't been entirely fair with Grace.

"No," he said finally. "I just ain't gabby."

"You've demonstrated that all week," she said tartly. "I've had to dig for everything, but now I've got my rope on you, or you've got yours on me, whichever way you want to say it."

It made a hell of a lot of difference to a man which way you said it, he thought. He forced himself to look at her. He saw the proud way she held her head, the little confident smile lingering at the corners of her mouth as if she had finally accomplished something she had set out to do.

"Grace, we might as well get this straight," he said. "I'm a small fry, I always will be, and I don't want to be anything else."

"Oh, you're talking crazy," she said impatiently. "Nobody wants to be small when he can have the moon if he reaches for it."

"I do," he said.

She was silent, apparently sensing that this was not the time to press the issue, and then suddenly he remembered what Karl Hermann had said the first day they had come to the valley. *She's always looking for men. She collects them.* Hermann had been warning him, but at the time he hadn't realized it.

When they stopped in front of the house Rod stepped down and gave her a hand. He saw Juan Herrera and Clay Cummings move toward them from the corral.

"There's Clay now, Grace," he said.

"Why, he looks just like I thought he would," she said. "His wife was a fool. After all this time, he's not beaten."

"A man like him never gets beaten." When Cummings came up, Rod said: "Clay, meet Grace Hermann. She's an admirer of yours."

Cummings took off his hat and stared at Grace, his face grave. "I reckon he's lying, ma'am. I'm an old horse put out on pasture, but nobody's got the guts to shoot me."

She laughed and held out a slim hand. "I know horses, Mister Cummings. I never saw a valuable horse get so old that he wasn't worth having around." She motioned toward the house. "You did a marvelous thing, coming here when you did. It wasn't fair for Daddy to take advantage of the work you did."

He took her hand, plainly surprised by what she said. Then he stepped back, still staring at her and frankly admiring her, a white-headed eagle of a man in whom the love of life was still a strong force.

"It wasn't a proposition of taking advantage, ma'am," he said. "Your dad was just a smart businessman." He wheeled to Rod, jerking his head toward the bunkhouse. "Let Juan take care of the horses. I want to talk to you."

Cummings strode across the yard to the bunkhouse. Rod glanced at Grace, who looked as if she had half a mind to follow him.

Rod said: "I'll see you at supper."

She laughed softly. "There goes a man. You bring him in for supper."

Rod nodded and caught up with Cummings. "Just ride in, Clay?"

"Last night." Cummings gave him a reproving glance. "You and the girl were out lollygagging, looks like."

"We got caught in the storm," Rod said.

Cummings snorted. "Wasn't that big a storm, boy. I didn't figure you were that soft in the head. Doll's your kind of woman, Rod. Take an old man's word for it who got run through a sausage grinder."

They went into the bunkhouse. Rod sat down and rolled a smoke. Cummings paced around like a nervous mountain lion. Finally he said: "I'm poking my nose into business that ain't mine, but I'm poking it anyhow. Why you don't put a hole in Jason Abbot's skull is something I can't understand."

"He hasn't given me a chance yet. He doesn't do his own fighting."

"Then run him out of the country," Cummings snapped. "He's a spider, a damned old spider working like hell on his web. He misfired that day you fetched the Hermanns to the valley, but he ain't done. They're cooking up something else, and I don't know what it is."

"They won't tackle Spade," Rod said. "Long as Hermann stays here, they can't hurt him."

"Don't be sure of that. They'll do something to fetch Hermann into town, and they'll fetch you too. Abbot is crazy, Rod. He won't rest till he gets you and Hermann, and Doll and Marcia are the ones who'll get hurt."

Rod finished his smoke and rolled another, sensing that the old man was having trouble saying what was in his mind.

Cummings sat down, and then got up again and began walking around the long room.

"I saw you smoke Barney Webb down," Cummings said. "You done good. I figured you'd slowed up, but I reckon that when a man learns to use a gun, he doesn't forget." He waggled a long, gnarled finger at Rod. "But you're mighty lucky to be alive. You know where Chuck England was?"

Rod shook his head. "I've been wondering."

"Upstairs in the hotel. He was in a front room facing the street, and he was gonna cut you down before you plugged Webb. Abbot schemed it out that way after you backed Kane and the rest of 'em down."

It tallied, Rod thought. He asked: "Well, why didn't he?"

"You chowder-headed idiot," Cummings shouted, "riding around with the Hermann girl and staying out all night with her! Hell's bells, you ain't got a lick of sense or you'd know why you were alive."

"All right," Rod said irritably. "I'm an idiot. Now tell me why I'm alive."

"Because Doll took a shotgun and went upstairs and held it on England till you was out of town . . . that's why. I got it out of Marcia, and I guess there was hell to pay afterward, when Abbot saw her."

Rod stared at the floor, unable to say anything, unable even to think coherently. Doll, who had cut everything off between them and accused him of wanting Grace, had saved his life. She wouldn't have done it if she hadn't loved him.

Rod looked at Cummings, utterly miserable. "She gave me my walking papers, Clay. She was done with me."

Cummings threw up his hands. "What you don't know about women would sure fill a book.

You gave her up mighty damned easy. If you really loved her, you'd . . ."

"All right," Rod said. "I'll go to town after supper."

Cummings laughed. "With Grace Hermann, I reckon."

Rod heard the triangle then, and rose. "You're eating in the house, Clay."

"I ain't doing no such thing."

"Grace's invitation. If you don't, she'll eat with you."

Cummings groaned. "To hell with stubborn women," he said, but he went along with Rod.

Hermann and George were in the living room. They spoke to Rod, making no mention of the night before, but George was glum, silent, and withdrawn, and Rod sensed his brother's deep anger. But Hermann was as friendly as ever. He wouldn't be shocked at all by anything Grace did.

After they had finished eating, Hermann leaned back in his chair and lighted a cigar. He said: "Clay, I need you. George won't let me leave Spade to see these fool settlers. Says it's dangerous."

"He's right," Cummings said.

"And Grace won't let me send Rod after them because that's dangerous."

"That's right, too."

Hermann pounded the table. "But I don't want

their half of the valley. If I could talk to them, I could make them believe me."

Cummings shook his head. "No, you couldn't. Not as long as Jason Abbot has 'em on the string. But I'll go see 'em. That's what you want, ain't it?"

"That's it," Hermann said. "I thought you could do it without stirring things up."

"Things'll stir the minute you hit town," Cummings said, "but maybe I can get Kane and some of 'em to come out here."

Hermann nodded and rose. "Rod, I want to talk to you in the office."

Hermann left the room. Rod's gaze touched Grace's face. She was smiling, the cool, confident smile that showed what was in her mind as clearly as spoken words. He swung around and left the dining room. When he reached the office, he saw that Hermann was sitting behind the desk, the swivel chair canted back.

"Sit down, Rod," Hermann said. "I'm not a man to beat around the bush. There was a time when I thought Grace and George would make a go of it. That suited me fine, because George is the kind of man I'd like for a son-in-law . . . but it won't work, because Grace has taken a shine to you."

"I can't . . ."

"I'm not done talking," Hermann interrupted. "Grace winds me around her finger. You've seen that already. I never try to figure out why she wants what she wants, but I try like hell to get it for her. She wants you. If she hasn't made that plain, I will."

"You told me once that she collected men."

"It's different with you. She's serious."

Rod sat down in a chair, thinking that for the first time since he had met Karl Hermann, the man was talking like a hundred million dollars. He had been used to buying anything Grace wanted, and because George had already been bought, Hermann assumed that Rod could be reached the same way.

"You don't know me very well," Rod said. "I like Grace . . ."

"Tell her, not me," Hermann said brusquely. "Maybe I don't know you very well, but I'm a businessman, and I've learned a few things. One of them is that if you don't grab what you want when you have a chance, you won't get anything when you do grab. Now this idea you've got of having your own place is crazy. I'm offering you a free ticket to anywhere you want to go."

Rod held back the angry words he felt like saying. Hermann was talking honestly, and it did not occur to him that Rod would hold to his purpose no matter how crazy it was.

"You started small," he said.

"Times were different," Hermann said. "The opportunities were big. Nowadays the open land is gone. You've got a ten-cow spread and that's all you'll ever have regardless of the trouble you're having with this Jason Abbot. Before I leave the valley, I'll figure out some way to whip Abbot, but that's neither here nor there."

"I started to say a few minutes ago that I like Grace too much to hurt her. I can't take that ticket you're offering me, and she wouldn't live with me on what I've got," Rod said.

Hermann leaned forward. "No, she wouldn't live on what you've got, but you're forgetting that I'm getting along in years. Won't be long until you'll fall into a bigger pile of money than you ever saw. Meanwhile, you can have any job in the organization."

"It would be Grace's money, not mine." Rod rose. "I'm sorry, but I can't do it. No sense trying to explain. It's just the way I feel."

"I'm the one who's sorry," Hermann said. "You're the right man for Grace. I saw that the day we were in Poplar City. You're different from George. I'm not running him down, because he's the kind of man I need . . . but you've got some of the same qualities I had when I was young and full of vinegar. You're tough enough to take my job over." He frowned, tapping the desk top, then asked: "It's not on account of your father and what I did, is it? I didn't know about that until it was wound up."

"No," Rod said. "I've changed my mind about

you. And about Grace. It's just that I know it wouldn't work out."

Someone was pounding on the front door.

Rod heard George say—"Come in,"—and then Doll's voice, asking: "Is Rod here?"

Rod went out of the office and into the living room in long strides. Doll was standing just inside the door, and in his first glance Rod saw that something was wrong. She was pale and scared and worried. When she saw Rod she started toward him.

He didn't have a chance to say anything he wanted to. Words poured out of Doll in an almost incoherent stream.

"Frank's in trouble, Rod. Abbot says you and Frank have been rustling calves, and the Ninety-Nine is going to hang you and him. They can't get hold of you, but they can him."

He caught her hands and was shocked when he discovered how cold they were. "You've seen Frank?" he asked.

She nodded. "I rode out there today, but he won't budge. You know how he is. He won't worry about anything for more than five minutes. He promised to leave until this blew over, but he was still there when I left."

"I'll see him tonight," Rod said.

"But that will give them a chance at you."

"I've handled Sam," Rod said. "I can handle him again."

"Rod!"

It was Grace's voice, peremptory and commanding. When he turned to her, he saw an expression of incredible shock on her face, as if she could not believe she was seeing him hold another woman's hands.

"Grace, this is Doll Nance," Rod said. "Doll, this is Grace Hermann."

George and Cummings were standing there, embarrassed and uneasy.

Doll said: "How do you do?"

But Grace made no pretense of greeting Doll. She walked toward Rod, her head held high. "I don't know what this is all about," Grace said in a shrewish tone, "but this girl had better leave."

"I guess I had," Doll said.

"I'm leaving with her," Rod said. "I've got a chunk of business that can't be put off."

"No you're not," Grace snapped. "You've got a job to do and it's here."

"That's right," George said. "You can't walk out . . ."

"I'll be back tomorrow," Rod said, and turned toward the door.

"Wait!" Hermann had come out of the office. He stared at Doll, his face as gray as weathered wood. A hand came up to his throat. "Marcia," he whispered, and then his knees buckled and he fell forward on his face.

Grace screamed. George ran to Hermann and

felt for his pulse, saying: "He's only fainted. Let's get him to the couch, Rod."

They lifted Hermann's limp body and carried him to the leather couch.

Grace cried: "It's his heart! He's got to have a doctor."

"There ain't a sawbones in the valley." Rod looked at George. "I can't do anything here. I've got to see Frank and then I'll be back."

He strode out of the room, ignoring Grace's pleading: "Rod . . . Rod, you can't go!"

He crossed to the corrals. He caught and saddled his horse, and when he stepped up, he saw that Grace was standing a few feet from him, her face haggard in the thin dusk light.

"I'm sorry about your dad," he said. "I hope he'll be all right."

"It isn't him, it's you," Grace cried. "Don't I mean anything to you?"

He looked down at her, knowing now that he didn't love her and never could. Even if he did, he could not change his attitude about going to work for Karl Hermann, and she would never change hers about being a nester's wife.

"It's her, isn't it?" Grace said bitterly, motioning toward Doll, who had mounted and was waiting by the poplars. "You're turning me down for her, aren't you?"

There was no trace now of the cool confidence which had so completely dominated her. She would not have wanted him in the first place, he thought, if he had been easy to get. He had challenged her without meaning to, and she had accepted that challenge.

"We were engaged," he said, "but Doll broke it off before you came to the valley. It isn't that, Grace."

He rode away, leaving her standing there staring after him.

Doll caught up with him as they crossed the bridge spanning Halfmile Creek.

"Why did Hermann call you Marcia?" he asked her.

"How should I know?" Doll said, staring straight ahead.

Well, maybe she didn't, Rod thought, so he changed the subject. "Clay told me you saved my life when I had the fight with Webb. I want to thank you, Doll."

"I'd have done it for anyone," she said indifferently.

Nothing had changed after all, he thought savagely. The wall between them was higher and wider than ever. If either of them broke it down, it would have to be him, and he doubted he could.

When they reached town, Doll said: "Put my horse in the stable, will you, and fetch Ma's mare back to the hotel. I'm going to Frank's place."

She had been coolly silent all the way from

Spade to Poplar City, showing him that she wanted nothing more to do with him, but that she liked Frank. She wouldn't have gone to Spade to get Rod if she hadn't thought he could shake Frank out of his inertia.

But she couldn't go. If this rumor about Kane's bunch was true, there would probably be a fight. Doll would be safer in town.

"You can't go," he said.

"I suppose you can keep me from going with you," she said evenly, "but you can't make me stay in town. I'm afraid something's happened to Frank, and I've got to find out."

"I'll let you know," he said.

"I'm going out there tonight, either with you or by myself."

They had reached Main Street, deserted and ominously quiet, and a moment later drew up in front of the hotel. "Ma wants to see you, Rod."

"I've got to go . . ."

"It won't take more than a minute," she broke in. "You owe her that much."

A man never escaped completely from the obligations he owed other people, Rod thought. But for Doll to say that he owed her mother anything was piling it on, and he started to tell her that when he remembered that Doll had saved his life. His debt was to her, not Marcia, but if she wanted him to see her mother, he would do it for her.

"All right," Rod said. Dismounting, he looped his reins over the hitch pole.

Doll rode on down the street toward the livery stable. She was going to get Marcia's mare herself, Rod thought.

Marcia was not in the lobby, but she must have heard him, for she came down the hall, calling: "That you, Rod?"

"Yeah, it's me." He paused at the desk, fighting his violent anger, and when Marcia reached him, he burst out: "Your fool girl's got the bit in her teeth and she's running with it. She wants to go with me to Frank's place. You better make her stay in town."

Marcia was as pale as she had been the day the Hermanns had come to the valley when he had talked to her in her parlor. But there was something else, too. She looked as if she had forgotten how to laugh, as if she had lived with an overpowering worry every day since Rod had seen her. Her hair was frowzy, her dress was wrinkled and dirty, and her eyes were red. She bore little resemblance to the self-possessed, pleasant woman he had known.

"Doll isn't a fool, Rod," Marcia said wearily. "She may be a lot of things, but she isn't a fool."

"What's wrong?" Rod asked.

"Everything. I've got the devil by the tail. I can't keep on running with him and I can't let go. I don't think you'll find Frank alive, but I couldn't think of anything else to do except to send Doll after you."

Rod gripped her arms. "How much do you know about this business?"

"Just what Doll's told you. This week has been hell. You backed Kane down and you killed Webb, and since then they've done nothing but scheme out how they were going to kill you."

"Just to get at Hermann?"

She nodded. "But it's more than that now. You've made a fool out of Jason. Now you've got to get out of the country. What's happened so far is just a beginning."

She jerked free of his grip and, stepping behind the desk, reached down and picked up a small sack filled with gold coins. "This is every cent I have, Rod. I want you to take Doll and leave the valley. Take Frank, if he's alive. It's enough for you to get a start somewhere else."

She held the sack out to him. He took it and set it on the desk. "You're not telling me all you know, Marcia."

"I've told you as much as I can," she cried. "You can't fight everybody, Rod. That's why I want Doll to go with you. Take Doll and get out before you're killed. For God's sake, take her if you love her."

Rod knew from the fear shadowing her face that it was Doll's future she worried about and this was the only thing she could do for her daughter.

"How did you know about Barney Webb the other day?"

She made a gesture, as if dismissing it lightly. "I know Jason."

"And you knew England would be upstairs waiting to shoot me in the back."

She nodded. "I suppose Clay told you about it. Doll had the idea of holding a gun on England. You owe her your life, Rod. Taking her out of the country is a small thing to do for the woman you want to marry. And don't tell me you've got to go on with your deal to protect Hermann. He's got plenty of men to do that."

He could not see why she was so concerned about him unless it was simply that she wanted him to stay alive so he could marry Doll. Well, she was wasting her hopes. Doll had made it as plain as a woman could that she was done with him.

"I'm sorry," Rod said. "I gave my word. I can't break it." He turned toward the door.

"Rod!" Marcia called, grabbing his arm and turning him to face her. "Rod, listen to me. You've hated Hermann for years, but you haven't let it poison you like it has me. This thing has just started. It isn't your fight and it isn't Doll's, but if you stay, you'll both get hurt."

"You hate Hermann. That it?"

"I didn't say . . ."

212

"He saw Doll tonight. He called her Marcia and fainted."

For a minute he thought Marcia was going to faint, too. She put a hand to her head and moved back to the desk to lean against it. "I don't know anything about that."

"I think you do. You ought to tell me."

She shook her head. "I can't. I'm not proud of myself anymore, Rod. There's just one decent thing left I can do for you and Doll."

Doll was waiting outside. He looked at Marcia, trembling and pale-faced, and he was certain that something out of her past had returned to plague her when Hermann had come to the valley, something she was too ashamed to tell him.

"We'll make out," he said shortly, and left the lobby.

He mounted his horse, saying nothing to Doll when she pulled in beside him. They left town at a fast pace, uneasiness over Frank's safety growing in him until it was close to panic.

They rode northwest, following the creek, and presently they began to climb as they reached the northern slope of the valley that tipped up toward the foothills. The thought that they might be riding into a trap grew in his mind. The accusation that he and Frank had rustled their neighbors' calves was so fantastic that only a sick mind like Jason Abbot's would ever have thought of it.

Rod found it hard to believe that Kane and Larkin and the rest of his neighbors would even give it a second thought. But he had beaten Kane that night in the Palace; he had backed the man down the day the Hermanns had come to the valley. Perhaps Abbot and England had framed him and Frank, by slapping the Rocking R and Frank's Bridlebit brand on a few calves. Kane, humiliated as he had been, might accept the evidence without question.

Half a mile below his hay meadow Rod said: "We'll turn off here."

Doll kept pace with him, saying nothing.

The mountains lifted directly ahead of them, pine-covered and black against the star-speckled sky. The country was lifting more sharply now, a few scattered trees around them, and a moment later Frank's cabin and shed made a vague shape in front of them.

"Rein up," Rod said in a low tone.

"They wouldn't stay around here if they've killed Frank," Doll whispered.

"You can't tell," Rod said.

For a long moment they sat there, listening and hearing nothing except the hooting of an owl far back in the timber.

Rod said: "Stay here. I'll have a look."

He stepped down, leaving his reins dangling, and moved silently toward the cabin, his right hand on his gun. He reached the front door of the cabin and shoved it open, standing to one side so he would not be silhouetted against the moonlight. The door made a spine-tingling squeal in the pressing silence—enough to wake Frank, if he were here. Rod slid through the door and put his back to the wall, his gun palmed. Still, no sound broke the silence.

"Frank," he called, suddenly realizing that Frank might be in the bunk and start shooting before he found out who was here.

The only answer was the echo of his own voice. He crossed to the bunk and put his hands on it. No one was there. He swung around, and as he stepped through the door, he heard Doll's scream from somewhere behind the cabin. She hadn't stayed where he'd told her to.

He swore and ran around the cabin, his heart hammering. He half expected to see gun flame blossom from the darkness, to hear the thunder of a shot, but he could not afford caution now. He tripped over Frank's chopping block and almost fell, then Doll cried out: "They hanged him, Rod."

He stopped. It seemed to him the earth was spinning out from under him, that this was a crazy nightmare and he would soon be waking up. Frank, indolent and careless, good-natured and easy-going, had never harmed anyone. Rod went on slowly; he saw the body dangling from a pine limb.

Rod holstered his gun. He stood there as Doll swung her horse toward him.

"It must have happened quite a while ago. He's cold," Doll told him.

"I'll get my horse," Rod said.

Now it didn't seem to make much difference whether anyone was around or not. He tramped down the slope to his sorrel and, mounting, rode back to the tree. He stood on the saddle and, taking his knife out of his pocket, slashed the rope and heard the body hit the ground soddenly.

Doll was crying softly. Rod stepped down and walked to the shed where Frank kept his shovel. He found it and returned to Doll. He was an automaton, impelled by the thought that he must bury Frank no matter who was watching, or what happened to him and Doll.

He dug the grave on the slope above the tree, thinking that Frank had always liked the view he had of the valley. He worked with savage intensity, remembering things that had happened, odd things like the poker games they had played, betting wildly until one of them owed the other thousands of dollars. Then they'd laughed and had a drink and forgotten it. He could hear Frank's laugh now, big and hearty, the kind of laugh that came from a man who liked to live.

Digging mechanically, Rod did not realize how deep he had gone until Doll said: "That's enough, Rod."

He climbed out of the hole, glancing up at the sky. He suddenly realized that dawn was at hand. He said: "I'll get something to wrap him in." He found a piece of tattered canvas in the shed and returned to the grave. He spread it beside the body, and it was then that he saw the paper pinned to Frank's shirt.

Doll was standing beside him. She asked: "What is it, Rod?"

He struck a match. The paper was a sheet torn from a tablet, the kind of tablet a kid would use in school. A blunt pencil had printed:

> This is a warning to all rustlers.
>
> The 99

He felt Doll's hand on his shoulder. He heard her whisper: "Maybe it wasn't the Ninety-Nine, Rod. Maybe it was just Abbot and Chuck England."

He didn't say anything. He rolled the body in the canvas, carried it to the grave, and lowered it as gently as he could. Then he filled the grave, and when the dirt was a round mound, he threw the shovel down, suddenly feeling his inadequacy.

Doll laid a hand on his arm, saying: "Except for you, I liked Frank better than any other man I ever knew."

Suddenly she began to cry, and he knew she

needed him as much as he needed her. He put his arms around her and she laid her head against his chest. They stayed that way for a long time, the light steadily deepening around them.

"I'll find out who did this," Rod said, "and I'll get them. I'll get every dirty son who had a hand in this."

Doll had stopped crying, but still she remained in his arms. Her voice was muffled when she said: "Don't make a mistake. That's what Abbot wants you to do."

He was silent for a time, wondering if Kane would tell him the truth. Finally he said: "We'd better go. Later on we'll put up a marker."

They walked downslope to their horses. Doll said in a low voice: "I've got to tell you something, Rod. I should have told you a long time ago, but I couldn't. Ma's to blame for this."

He looked at her, shocked by what she said. "That's crazy."

"No, not when you know what's happened. When Hermann bought Spade, she knew that sooner or later he'd come here. She wanted to break him, kill him, anything to get even. So she started telling Abbot what a great man he could be . . . as great as Hermann, if he had the valley. He believed her. That's why he's done the things he has. He thinks you'll kill Kane and then everybody will hunt you till they catch you."

"But it's Hermann . . ."

"Remember what happened in town the day Hermann got here? Abbot knows that's the way it will be. He can't get Hermann until he gets you."

He stared at her in the thin light, sensing that even her love for her mother was not enough to silence her now. Then it didn't seem so crazy. He'd had the feeling that Marcia hadn't been entirely honest with him. Frank had paid for her revenge. Marcia hadn't cared about that, but she didn't want Doll and Rod to pay, too.

"Why does she hate Hermann?" Rod asked.

"She used to be Hermann's girl, before I was born. She expected him to marry her, but he found someone else he cared about more, so he left her. She was awfully young then. I guess it's natural that she'd hate him."

Doll looked like Marcia when she was a girl, and Hermann, not knowing she was here, had been hit hard by that resemblance. He must have thought that the years had been rolled back and Marcia was standing before him. But all of this didn't really change anything.

He said: "We'd better ride."

He gave her a hand and she stepped into the saddle. He mounted, trying to decide what to do. There was no sense in going to Kane now. That was plainly what Abbot expected. But it was Abbot he had to find, Abbot and England. They might be at their ranches, or in town.

He heard a shout. He heard Doll cry out: "Rod, they're coming!"

He stared downslope through the pines. The morning light was still very thin, but he saw the horsemen, three of them, and although they were too far away for him to be sure, he thought one of them was Abbot. His first impulse was to ride straight toward them and have it out now, then he knew he couldn't. Three to one were long odds. With Doll to look out for they were impossible.

"We'll make a run for it," he said, and whirled his horse upslope.

A rifle cracked, the slug missing Rod by inches, then they were in the thick timber and for the moment they were safe. There would be no help from anyone.

Rod was the one they wanted, not Doll. He shouted: "We'll split! You head for Kane's SK and I'll go the other way."

"I won't do it!" she cried. "Whatever happens to you will happen to me."

He swore and, glancing back, glimpsed them entering the timber. Again a rifle shot smashed into the mountain silence, the bullet knocking bark from a pine trunk beside him. Damn Doll's stubbornness! He had foreseen this, but he hadn't been able to do anything about it.

The sun was showing now, throwing long banners of golden light through the pines. The slope ran on for another hundred yards to the top of the ridge. Rod knew this country so well he could draw a map of it from memory. A cañon lay beyond the ridge, a brush-choked stream at the bottom. If they dropped into it, they would be slowed down and eventually trapped.

Rod had only his six-gun in his holster. Abbot's bunch had at least one Winchester. Any way he looked at it, the situation was so bad it was fatal if he stopped to make a fight.

Doll would be safe if he got her to Poplar City, or to Spade. But both places were miles away, so many miles that he might as well forget them. They had to turn one way or the other when they reached the top of the ridge. If he went west, he might be able to keep ahead of them long enough to swing downslope to his cabin, but that would mean a siege. With no possibility of help, they would get him sooner or later, perhaps burn him out, or wait until thirst drove him into the open.

If he turned the other way, he would be in Kane's and Larkin's country. Nothing would please them better than to get their hands on him. But Doll would be safe, and at this moment nothing else seemed important. He'd have to take his chances.

"We'll swing east!" he called when they reached the top of the ridge.

"You'll run into Kane and his bunch!" Doll yelled back.

"I aim to!" he shouted.

He turned his horse, and Doll followed unwillingly. They had no time to blow their horses, but now they weren't climbing. The air was dry and cool. Hoofs dug into the thick mat of pine needles, dust drifting back behind them.

They crossed an open place, reaching the east end just as Abbot's bunch came into view. Now, with the full daylight upon them, Rod saw that it was England and Shannon who were with Abbot, Shannon in the rear. England was in front, a rifle across his saddle horn, and he let go with another shot that was close.

The timber closed around them again, so thick that their pursuers had only an occasional glimpse of them. Rod swung downhill, angling eastward so that he would come out of the pines just above Kane's place.

"You're jumping out of the frying pan into the fire!" Doll shouted. "This is crazy!"

He went on, taking a twisting route through the trees. Maybe it was crazy, but Doll would be safe once she was in Kane's cabin. They hit another open space, the timber forming a dark wall on both sides, and they were barely out of it when their pursuers reached the upper end. England fired again, the bullet coming closer to Doll than Rod.

"Watch where you're shooting!" Abbot bellowed.

He wouldn't want Doll hurt. Then the thought

struck Rod that maybe he had no reason to be worried about Doll, since she was Marcia's daughter, and Abbot and Marcia . . . It wasn't any good. Rod knew that at once. Not with Abbot the kind of man he was. Besides, the chance of her getting tagged by a stray slug was too big for him to make a fight of it.

They rode recklessly, zig-zagging through the trees, the ground uneven and strewn with limbs. They jumped their horses over a windfall, Rod thinking that if one of their mounts went down, it would be the finish for them. A moment later they came into the open, the slant not so steep here. Kane's place was directly below them.

Two men were standing in front of the cabin. One would be Kane, Rod thought, and Larkin would probably be the other.

Rod called: "The minute we get to Kane's cabin, you hike inside. You hear me?"

"I'm listening, but I don't hear," she said defiantly. "What do you think you're doing besides committing suicide?"

They were halfway between the fringe of timber and the cabin when Abbot's bunch came into view. Rod pulled his gun and threw a shot back at them. It was a waste of lead because the distance was too great, but it might slow them down.

Rod glanced at Doll's white, drawn face. She was staring at the cabin, and when Rod looked at it, he saw that the two men had seen them and one had run inside. England's rifle cracked, the bullet fanning Rod's cheek. The man who had gone inside was standing in the doorway, a rifle in his hands, and now that he was closer, Rod saw that it was Clay Cummings. Relief swept through him. They'd be all right.

Cummings threw the Winchester to his shoulder and began firing. Rod and Doll were on the grass now, with only a few scattered pines around them. They swept past Kane's corrals and the log shed and reined their heaving horses up in front of the cabin, dust swirling around them.

"Look at them yellow devils run!" Cummings shouted. "Look at 'em, Sam. Your friend Abbot don't cotton to an even fight."

Rod looked back. The three men had wheeled their mounts and were heading back into the timber.

Cummings put his rifle down and glared at Rod. "Of all the chuckle-headed idiots, you take the cake with the pink icing. What'd you get Doll into this scrape for?"

Doll slid out of the saddle. She wiped a hand across her dust-smeared face, trembling, then she said: "Don't blame him, Clay. He couldn't do anything about it."

"Well, I could have," the old man snapped. "Even if I had to tie you up."

Rod stepped down and looked at Kane, who was

eying him coldly. He was afraid, Rod thought, now that he was alone, for he knew Cummings would do nothing for him. Still, Kane stood rooted there, held by his natural stubbornness. Rod felt some admiration for the man. He wasn't a coward. He thought Rod was going to kill him, but he wouldn't beg.

Mrs. Kane stepped out of the cabin. "Doll," she said, as if not quite sure she could believe what she saw, "was that Abbot who was chasing you?" When Doll nodded, Mrs. Kane swung to her husband. "Sam, what kind of a man would do a thing like that?"

Kane's face was red. He stood with his thick legs spread, right hand close to his gun, eyes on Rod.

Cummings said: "It proves what I've been telling Sam, Missus Kane. One of these days he'll wake up."

"He can do it now and fetch you all in for breakfast," she said tartly. "It's time he quit this riding and gabbing and scheming. You hear me, Sam?"

"Just a minute, Missus Kane," Rod said. "Sam, you're not smart or you wouldn't have let Abbot get you into this. But I'll say one thing for you. I never knew you to lie."

Kane's lips sneered. "I'm supposed to thank you for a compliment, I reckon."

"No, I'm just saying I'll believe you when you

answer a question, but it's only fair to tell you I'll kill you if your answer is yes. Did you or Larkin or any of your Ninety-Nine bunch lynch Frank Benson?"

Kane's mouth came open in sheer surprise. "He was lynched?"

Rod handed him the sheet of paper he had taken from Frank's body. "We just finished burying him when Abbot showed up. This was pinned on his shirt."

Kane stared at it, an expression of horror creeping into his square face. "None of us had anything to do with it. You've got to believe that."

Rod took the paper out of his hand and stuffed it into his pocket. "I had a hunch it was Abbot's doings, Sam. It's time you and me was working together instead of fighting."

"I told him that," Cummings said.

"I'm going to kill Abbot," Rod said. "How do you stand on this, Sam?"

"We won't stop you." Kane scowled at Cummings. "Maybe you're right about Hermann. Maybe we were suckers to listen to Abbot in the first place."

Cummings's face broke into a grin. "That's the first smart thing you've said since I got here." Cummings looked at Rod. "I asked Sam to get his bunch together and meet Hermann in town."

"All right," Kane said as if still uncertain about this. "We'll be on hand tomorrow, but Abbot . . ."

"I'll take care of him," Rod said. "Just be sure he knows about the meeting. It'll shove him into the open where I can get at him. That's all I want."

"If you don't get in here to breakfast," Mrs. Kane said, "I'm going to throw it out."

"Go on in," Kane said. "I'll take care of the horses."

It was a silent meal, with Kane's face showing he had not been entirely convinced. Rod doubted that Hermann could say anything that would change Kane's and his neighbors' fear. It had been in them too long, planted and watered by Abbot's sly words—so long that now even if they broke with Abbot, the chances were that they would still suspect Hermann of trickery.

When they had finished eating, Rod told Doll: "I'm taking you back to Spade with me. It's safer than town."

He didn't think she was in any danger, but he wanted Hermann to see her again.

Mrs. Kane scowled at Rod. "You're loco if you don't let her rest. If you had an eye in your head, you'd see she was played out."

"You could stand a little snooze yourself," Cummings said to Rod. "I'll ride back with you while Sam takes a pasear around the valley and rounds up his neighbors. But we ain't in no hurry."

Doll tried to smile, weariness showing in the droop of her shoulders. "I'll lie down for an hour, Rod, but I think I ought to go to town."

Cummings had sensed what was in Rod's mind. He said quickly: "We'd best stay the night at Spade. Marcia will be all right."

Doll, not feeling like arguing, nodded and let it go. Rod went outside and stretched out in the shade of the cabin. He was asleep at once, and when Cummings shook him awake, he found it hard to believe he had been asleep at all.

"Time we was moving," Cummings said. "I know what you're thinking about Hermann and Doll. I got Marcia to talking three, four days ago, and I know a little bit about what happened. Doll tell you?"

Rod nodded. "Did Hermann come out of it after we left?"

"Yeah, he's all right, but Grace was scared to death. Hermann wouldn't talk in front of her and I had to leave because I wanted to get up here last night. I didn't find out anything from him, but I've got the same hunch you have."

Rod rose stiffly. "We'd best ride if Doll's awake."

They made a slow ride to Spade, hitting the creek two miles above Poplar City. Because Doll was worried about her mother, Cummings left them and went into town. He caught up with them when they struck the road as it bent south around the lake.

"Your ma's all right," Cummings told Doll. "She's mighty sorry to hear about Frank, but she's glad you and Rod made it."

The sun was far down in the west when they reined up beside the poplars. Juan Herrera came toward them, giving them his toothy grin. Rod would have helped with the horses if George had not called from the house: "Rod, Mister Hermann wants to see you. You, too, Clay."

When they went into the house, Rod saw that Hermann was lying on the couch, a quilt over him. Grace was seated beside him. She rose, angry eyes on Doll.

"What's she doing back here, Rod?"

"I don't have to stay . . . ," Doll began.

"She's welcome here," Hermann said harshly. "Go upstairs, Grace."

Grace hesitated, her face shrewish in the slanting sunlight coming through the open door. Suddenly she whirled and crossed the room to the stairs. She climbed them, her heels striking each step sharply.

"Any luck, Clay?" Hermann asked.

"They'll be in town tomorrow morning at ten," Cummings answered.

"They'll listen to me. There won't be any trouble." Hermann fixed his eyes on Doll, smiling a little. "Come here."

He was sick, Rod thought, and his years had caught up with him. Doll hesitated, then reluctantly moved to the couch. Reaching out, Hermann took her hand. He said softly: "Doll, I have every reason to think that you are my daughter."

Doll jerked her hand as if repelled by what he had said and ran to Rod. He put his arms around her and shook his head at Hermann. He said: "We were damned near killed this morning. Now we're tired and hungry and mighty near the end of our twine."

"Who would want to kill you?" Hermann asked incredulously.

"Abbot and Chuck England." Rod looked at George. "And Todd Shannon."

George's face was expressionless. "I'll have Wang fix something for you to eat," he said, and left the room.

Hermann moistened his colorless lips with the tip of his tongue. "Doll, I didn't know your mother was here. I hurt her a long time ago. Maybe I can make it up to her now."

Doll drew away from Rod, her eyes hating Hermann. She said with biting contempt: "I'm not your daughter. Let my mother alone."

Hermann sat up. "I would be the last person to

defend myself, but I have the right to try to make amends."

"How can anyone make amends for a thing like that?" Doll cried.

Rod put an arm around her waist. "Talk to her in the morning," he said to Hermann, and led her into the dining room.

Rod went to the bunkhouse as soon as he had eaten, George promising to take Doll upstairs to a bedroom. He'd see to it that Grace didn't bother her. They'd talk it out in the morning.

Cummings woke him at dawn. "You're done sleeping," Cummings said excitedly. "We've got more trouble than you ever dreamed about. Marcia said Abbot had an ace up his sleeve, but she didn't say what it was. Maybe she didn't know."

Rod put his feet on the floor, his mind still foggy with sleep. "What are you talking about?"

"Somebody blowed the sand reef last night, and water's pouring through the hole like a millrace. We'll have that marginal land on the edge of the lake exposed and Abbot and his bunch will move in. What do you think Hermann's gonna do?"

Cummings's words swept the fog from Rod's mind. So that was Jason Abbot's ace! There would be hell to pay now.

IV

Rod buckled his gun belt around him, put on his hat, and went outside to the horse trough. He washed his face, thinking that whatever chance there had been of getting the small ranchers to listen to Hermann was gone. They'd leave their places to grab the marginal land, and Hermann wouldn't stand for that.

"Did you wake George?" Rod asked.

"He's up," Cummings answered. "He said he'd wake Hermann."

They turned toward the house. Rod asked: "How'd you find out?"

"Something woke me," Cummings said. "I thought I heard an explosion, so I got my horse and crossed the bridge. Hell, I was in water up to my horse's belly before I knew it."

A lamp had been lighted in the living room, and Rod went into the house as Hermann was coming down the stairs, his hair disheveled.

Hermann yawned and shook his head. "Hell of a time to get up." He saw Cummings behind Rod. "What's all this about, Clay?"

"You've got trouble," Cummings said. "It's up to you now."

George called from the dining room door.

232

"Wang's got coffee ready! He'll have breakfast in a minute!"

Hermann tramped across the living room, calling over his shoulder: "George says somebody blew a channel in the sand reef."

"That's right," Cummings said. "Won't be long till you have a few thousand acres of new land in the valley, and as soon as Kane hears it, the little fry will move onto it. That's why I said it's up to you."

Hermann sat down at the table and drank the scalding coffee that the cook had placed before him. He wiped a hand across his mouth. "One way to wake up is to boil your gullet." He yawned again. "Well, I don't see anything to this. The land's mine. I own the lake shore. Wouldn't be any question about the lake bottom that's exposed. Ever hear of riparian rights, Clay?"

"Yeah, I've heard of it, but legal shenanigans ain't gonna settle this." Cummings had sat down across from Hermann. "I've been willing to help out just to keep a fight from boiling up, but now I'm out of it. I ain't got no axe to grind." He nodded at Rod. "You talk to him, Rod."

"I don't have any axe, either," Rod said. "I'm satisfied with the Rocking R. I was hired to protect Hermann, but if he's bent on making a fight, I'm out of it, too."

"But, damn it, the land's mine."

"Mister Hermann," George said mildly, "the question isn't who owns the land. The courts will decide that in time, and I'm not sure you can make your claim stick."

"I know I can," Hermann said hotly. "As long as I own the shoreline, any lake bottom that's exposed belongs to me."

Wang brought a platter of flapjacks and bacon and padded back into the kitchen for the coffee pot.

George said: "Rod, tell him what we're up against."

This was as good a time as any to have it out with George, Rod thought. He pinned his eyes on his brother. "You didn't tell me all there was to tell when you hired me."

Startled, George said: "What didn't I tell you?"

"About Todd Shannon."

Hermann looked up from his plate. "What's this?"

George was staring at Rod, momentarily shaken. He said in a low tone: "Before I hired Rod, I made a deal to buy information from Shannon. I had to know what was going on in the valley, and it was the only way I could get it."

"But Shannon would sell his own mother out for a dime," Rod said bitterly. "You think you could trust him?"

George shrugged. "It was the best I could do. With Mister Hermann coming to the valley, I had to do something. At the time, I wasn't certain you'd take the job I offered you."

Rod let it go, not sure he could believe George, but this was not the time to push it. He turned to Hermann. "It's up to you, as Clay said. If you want a fight, you'll get it if you try to keep Kane and his bunch from moving onto the marginal land. Words won't convince them you want to be a good neighbor. Actions will. You tell these men they're welcome to settle on land you don't need, and you'll make friends. Otherwise, you'd best call your boys in off the range, give them guns, and tell them to kill every man who crosses your north line."

Hermann pounded the table. "I won't just hand them land that belongs to me. The day we came to the valley I saw what the situation was. With that marginal land drained and planted to grass, I can double my herd."

Silence fell while the rest ate. Hermann looked around the table, his face red and stubborn, then slowly the color drained out of it. "I'm a sick man," he said. "I might as well admit it. Seeing Doll the other night knocked my legs out from under me. I don't want a fight."

"The boys will be in Poplar City by ten o'clock," Cummings said. "I'm telling you once more. It's up to you."

"I've heard a lot of hogwash from you and Grace," Rod said to Hermann. "About your principle of avoiding trouble even if it cost you money. I reckon that's all it was . . . just hogwash."

"Let them have it, Mister Hermann," George urged. "Abbot was counting on you to claim the land or he wouldn't have blown a channel in the reef. He'll be in town at that meeting and he'll tell them to fight."

"This time they'll do it," Rod said. "I forced Kane and his boys to back down the other day, but I won't even try this time. As long as I've been in the valley I've heard talk about what would happen if the reef went out. Now it will happen, regardless of Jason Abbot."

Rod went back to eating, but he realized his appetite had gone. He was surprised that George was siding with him in this. He was even more surprised when George said: "Mister Hermann, I know what it is to be a poor man and want to get ahead. Rod knows it better than I do because he had the guts to make his own way. I wish I had."

Hermann said: "George, you've got everything."

"Not everything," George said harshly. "Rod and me didn't get along because he was as independent as a hog on ice and I liked to have some icing on my cake. But one thing is sure. If you're so damned greedy you're going to hold this marginal land that you don't need, you'd better start looking for a new superintendent for Spade."

"You know, George," Rod said, "from now on we're gonna get along. I'll give you a job on the Rocking R."

George gave him a tight grin. "I'll keep that in mind."

Rod rolled a smoke, his eyes on Hermann. "There's one thing you'd better know now. I can't tell you whether Doll is your daughter or not. All I know is you've done a hell of a thing to Marcia. We've been blaming Abbot for kicking up this trouble, but Marcia was the one who did the job. She wants to knock you down a peg or two, and I think she's gonna do it."

Cummings rose and kicked back his chair. "I'll get along home. Go ahead and have your fight." He walked out.

Rod struck a match and lit his cigarette, watching Hermann's hands grip the table so tightly that his knuckles were white.

Finally, Hermann said: "The land ain't worth it. Nothing's worth it. I have never knowingly caused a man's death. I won't now."

"Then you've got just one thing to do," Rod said. "Be in town by ten this morning and tell Kane they can have this land if they want it. It's the only way you can cut the ground away from Abbot and Marcia."

"What are you going to do?" Hermann asked.

"I'm going after Abbot. What's between him and me has nothing to do with your end of it."

"I'll go with you," George said.

Rod shook his head. "You'd best fetch Hermann in. Bring Doll, too. I've done wrong, bringing her out here with Marcia feeling like she does."

Rod started toward the living room. Hermann had not said definitely that he would give up the land, but Rod was sure he would. He had learned during the days he had been on Spade that there was an innate sense of decency in Hermann he didn't believe existed before taking this job. It was not greed that stopped Hermann now, he thought, for it was a natural impulse for a man to hold what he believed to be his.

Before Rod reached the door Hermann said: "Devers."

Rod turned. Hermann was still clutching the table, his head bent. Rod said: "Well?"

"I won't fight them. I'll be in town by ten, and I'll tell them so."

"Then you'll make a lot of friends," Rod said, and went on out of the house.

The sun was showing now, and as Rod caught and saddled his sorrel, he thought about Hermann, wondering if his sense of guilt over the way he had treated Marcia was the main factor in making up his mind. Or was it his principle of avoiding trouble? Not that, Rod decided, or he never would have reached the place he had. No, it must be Marcia, and then seeing Doll the other night and mistaking her for Marcia. Whatever happened now, Karl Hermann would not be the same man he had been when he had come to Spade.

He crossed the bridge, surprised by the volume of water that was pouring through the reef and running over the dike. He put his horse through it and reached the dry road on the other side. Then he brought his sorrel up to a faster pace and pulled his hat brim down as he turned east along the north shore of the lake and faced the sun.

There was no way to tell what would happen in town. Abbott would see to it that Kane knew about the break in the reef, and he would do his best to convince Kane that only a fight would win the marginal land. It was choice land, once it was drained and sowed to grass, but it meant moving from where they were. They were better off if thcy stayed where they were, but they wouldn't see that. They had wanted the lake bottom too long.

Rod thought of Frank Benson, who had been murdered for no good reason except that Jason Abbot had believed it was the one way he could get Rod. But he had failed.

The road swung north and presently the buildings of Poplar City appeared ahead of him, a pathetic huddle here in the vast ocean of grass. Abbot would be in town. Well, there was only one thing now that could be done. Whatever happened, Abbot would die.

Rod rode into town slowly. Main Street was deserted except for a dog sleeping in the dust. It was not yet ten. Kane and his bunch had not arrived, but they would come. It would be better, Rod thought, if he could take care of Abbot before they got here.

Rod reined up in front of the hotel and dismounted. He tied his sorrel, his eyes on Abbot's office. The door was shut, but Abbot might be inside. If he were, Chuck England would probably be with him. Maybe Todd Shannon, too. He stood beside his sorrel for a moment, staring at Abbot's office, caution working in him.

The shot smashed into the silence, somewhere in the back of the hotel. Rod had forgotten about Marcia. He ran into the empty lobby and saw Ada Larkin's scared face peering around the jamb of the dining room door.

"Abbot been around?" Rod demanded.

She nodded, swallowing, and pointed down the hall toward Marcia's parlor. He sprinted down the hall, his gun in his hand. The door was open. He lunged through it, expecting to see Abbot, but the man wasn't there. Marcia lay on the floor, blood making a scarlet spot on her dress just below her left shoulder. A small gun was clutched in her right hand.

He knelt beside her, saying her name softly. She was alive, and recognized him. "Who did it?" he asked her.

"Abbot," she whispered. "Funny the way things like this work out, Rod. I wouldn't be here if I hadn't poisoned myself hating Hermann. I'm glad you were big enough not to. You had something else to work for. I didn't."

"Let me get you into bed."

"It's too late, Rod." She reached for his hand and gripped it. "Listen, Rod."

"I'm listening."

"You and Doll are young and foolish, but you're in love. I know, Rod. I've known for a long time. Don't let your crazy pride keep you apart. Promise me you'll take care of her."

He was too choked up to say anything for a moment. He had always liked Marcia. Now she was dying and there was nothing he could do.

"I promise," he said.

Up there at Frank's place, Doll had said: *Except for you, I liked Frank better than any other man I ever knew.* Now, looking at Marcia's pain-wracked face, he knew there was nothing that could keep him and Doll apart.

Marcia's hand slid away from his. "I tried to kill Abbot this morning. That's why he shot me. I created a monster out of a vain man. A crazy one, too, I guess, although I didn't know that when I started. I tried to destroy him. God forgive me.

I never thought I'd bring so much misery to so many people just by trying to get even with Hermann."

She smiled a little. "There's one more thing. Jason is in love with Doll. Oh, I was good enough for him until he began dreaming his big dreams. Then he said he had to have a young wife and he was crazy enough to think he could make Doll love him. That's why he tried so hard to get rid of you. He knew he could never have her as long as you were around."

"Marcia, is Doll Hermann's daughter?"

Her eyes came open. "No. After Hermann left me I married a man named Ted Nance. Hermann was a widower then, and I had big dreams, dreams as foolish as Jason's. After I found out how it was, I married the first man I could get. He died a year later and I've had to fight for a living ever since." Her eyes closed again. She reached out for his hand and squeezed it. "Rod, be good to her."

A moment later she was gone. Rod picked her up and carried her into her bedroom across the hall. Ada Larkin was watching from the lobby.

He stopped as he passed her. "She's dead," he said. "Who takes care of things like this?"

"Missus Grout," the girl whispered. "I'll get her." She ran past him, her head bent.

Rod went on across the lobby into the street and stood motionless in front of the hotel, the morning sun sharp and bright on the white dust.

Marcia Nance had created a monster and then had tried to destroy him. Rod ran the tip of his tongue over the roof of his mouth. The monster had destroyed her. But if anybody was to blame it was Karl Hermann.

Hermann had changed. Perhaps a sense of guilt had laid against his heart through the years, and that guilt might be the answer to why he had been willing to give up land which he considered legally his. It was too late to alter things. All he could do was to go the whole way to keep others from being hurt.

Suddenly Rod was aware that George was driving a buggy in from the south, Hermann in the seat beside him, Doll and Grace riding beside the buggy. Telling Doll about Marcia would be the hardest thing Rod had ever had to do.

Kane and his friends were riding in, too. Abbot was hiding somewhere in town, Rod thought. Studying the band of incoming riders, he could see neither England nor Todd Shannon. They would be with Abbot.

The buggy wheeled up to the front of the hotel. Doll must have seen the misery in Rod's face, for she stepped down and ran to him.

She whispered: "What happened?"

He took her hands and held them tightly. "Steady now," he said softly. "Your mother's dead. Abbot shot her."

She looked at him, her mind gripping what he had said, and he wondered if she had sensed it before he had told her. She was too shocked to cry. She asked: "Where is she?"

"In her bedroom."

Doll walked past Rod into the hotel. Rod nodded at Grace who still sat her saddle, entirely unconcerned about this. She said quite casually: "George and I are getting married. Some men are smart enough to reach for the moon when it's offered them."

He felt like slapping her. "Doll could use you now," he said. "See if you can do anything."

She stiffened. "There's nothing . . ."

"Go inside," Rod said.

Hermann got out of the buggy, his face hard set. Grace wasn't twisting him around her finger now. "Do what he says. You can do a decent thing once in your life."

Rod had been wrong about her, he thought, for she had been posing all week and he had given her credit she did not deserve. Not once had he seen her the way she really was. He felt a sudden pity for George as Grace reluctantly swung down and walked into the hotel.

George tied the team, saying to his brother: "Looks like this is it, Rod. Will they talk?"

"I'll see that they do," Rod answered.

Kane and his men were in the street not more than half a block away. Yesterday Kane had been of a mind to listen, but today his square face held the old familiar stubbornness. They were armed just as they had been the day the Hermanns had come to the valley, but there was a difference about them, an intangible difference but a very real one. The idea that they could get what they wanted without a fight was far from their minds.

Rod stepped into the street, knowing that this moment would tell the story. He called out: "You heard about the sand reef going out?"

"You're damned right we've heard." Kane pulled up and raised his rifle to cover Hermann. "And we heard about you wanting to be neighborly, Hermann, but that was before you knew the reef had gone out."

"I still want to be neighborly." Hermann faced them, his shoulders back, showing the courage George had said was in him. "I wanted to talk to you ever since I've been here, but . . ."

"Talk!" Kane yelled. "To hell with it! We want land, good land that belongs to them that needs it and not a damned millionaire. . . ."

"He ain't figuring on stopping you, Sam," Rod broke in.

Kane's mouth fell open. Hermann said quickly: "If you boys want the lake bottom, move onto it. I'm going back to San Francisco, but I'm leaving orders with George Devers to give you any assistance you need."

He was talking loudly, so loudly that anyone along the street could hear. Now the batwings of the Palace slammed open and Jason Abbot came out. It was the last thing Rod expected. He had supposed he'd have to hunt the man down, but Abbot had heard what Hermann said. He had played his ace when he had blown the channel in the reef, but his ace wasn't the high card. Now, with the roof falling in on him, he was making his last desperate play.

"Kill him, Sam!" Abbott screamed at Kane. "You'll never get that land as long as Hermann's alive. He's lying to you. Kill him."

England and Shannon appeared behind Abbot. Now England's hand swept downward for his gun butt. A shot hammered out from somewhere behind Rod as he made his draw, the bullet knocking England back against the saloon wall. Abbot had pulled a gun, too, but whether he intended shooting Rod or Hermann was a question.

Abbot's gun swung up, but he didn't fire it. Rod shot him before he could squeeze the trigger. Abbot spun and fell. England braced against the wall, brought his gun up again. A second shot roared from behind Rod, and England's feet slid out from under him as he sprawled full out on the board walk.

Rod ran toward them, shouting: "Shannon!"

Todd Shannon leaped toward the batwings.

Rod let go with another shot that splintered the edge of one of the swinging doors, and Shannon stopped and threw up his hands.

"All right, all right! I'm out of it!" he yelled, and backed along the walk and stood with his hands over his head. He was sweating and trembling and his lips were quivering, a coward begging for his life.

"Shut up," Rod said, "unless you can think of one reason why I shouldn't kill you. You helped murder Frank."

"No I didn't," Shannon squealed. "It was Abbot and England. I busted the fence around your spring and I done a lot of little ornery things because Abbot said you'd leave the country, but I didn't have anything to do with the hanging."

"That's right." Abbot lay on his back, a trickle of blood running down his chin. "You've got nothing against Shannon."

Rod stared down at the dying man. He was surprised that now with the string run out, he didn't hate Jason Abbot as he had a few minutes before. It was justice, if a man could call it that, but a poor kind of justice that could not undo what had been done. Rod raised his eyes to Shannon.

"Maybe you're too big a coward ever to help a man." Rod thought of Shannon's family. Killing him would accomplish nothing. "You've got till sunset to get out of the valley, and if I ever hear of you letting your family starve, I'll hunt you up and finish you."

"I'll take care of them," Shannon cried, and ran down the street and disappeared around a corner.

For some reason Rod thought of what Marcia had said about letting her hate destroy her. Hate could do that, but hate was an honest feeling compared to the greed and vanity and crazy pride that had dominated Jason Abbot. He swung around and left Abbot there, and it was then that he saw the gun in George's hand. George had been the one who had downed England.

Red gave his brother a tight grin. "I wasn't fast enough to get both of them and there wasn't anybody else who'd have helped." George's searching eyes were on him, seeking approval, and he added: "I didn't know you could handle a gun."

"I can when I have to." George held out his hand. "Rod, I never meant anything more in my life than what I said that day about not having any kin but you."

"It'll be different now," Rod said. "You sticking with Hermann?"

"I have to. He's going to be my father-in-law. I've been in love with Grace as long as I've known her. I can't help it, Rod."

"Good luck," Rod said, and went to the hotel, knowing how it was. Some women did that to a man. Some like Doll were worthy of a man's love, and others like Grace weren't, but it made no difference when a man felt the way George did.

Hermann and the others were moving toward the front of the Palace. It was finished, Rod thought, the page turned. He was done with the Hermanns. He wanted to tell Karl Hermann that he was to blame for all of this, but nothing would be gained by it. Hermann must know that.

Grace was sitting in the lobby. When Rod came in, she said with the contempt of a woman who feels her superiority: "Doll doesn't need anyone but you. You're two of a kind. Nesters."

"George is a good man," Rod said, and knew at once it was a foolish thing to say to Grace who would not be impressed with goodness. "Tell your father Doll is not his daughter."

He went past Grace and along the hall, knowing that was one thing she'd be glad to hear.

The door of Marcia's parlor was open. Doll was standing at the window. Now, hearing Rod come in, she turned, steeling herself against the grief she felt. The tears had not started yet. She held out a slip of paper.

"I found this on the floor. Ma must have written it after she was shot."

Rod looked at it. One line written in a shaky hand. **Doll, listen to your heart.** That was all. Rod put his hands on the girl's arms. "She said something like that to me before she died, only it was about pride. It's hard for a man like me to crawl, but I will crawl if that's what I've got to do. I love you, Doll. I always have, but there's one difference. It'll be on your terms, if you'll have me."

"Terms aren't important, Rod," she said in a low tone. "They used to be, but not now. It's just you I want."

He put his arms around her and held her so that her face was against his shirt. She began to cry. She would feel better for it, he thought. He had come a long way since Hermann's bank had taken over his father's ranch, a very long way, but he had come alone. That was the big difference. He wouldn't be alone now.

ABOUT THE AUTHOR

Wayne D. Overholser won three Spur Awards from the Western Writers of America and has a long list of fine Western titles to his credit. He was born in Pomeroy, Washington, and attended the University of Montana, University of Oregon, and the University of Southern California before becoming a public schoolteacher and principal in various Oregon communities. He began writing for Western pulp magazines in 1936 and within a couple of years was a regular contributor to Street & Smith's *Western Story Magazine* and Fiction House's *Lariat Story Magazine*. *Buckaroo's Code* (1947) was his first Western novel. In the 1950s and 1960s, having retired from academic work to concentrate on writing, he would publish as many as four books a year under his own name or a pseudonym, most prominently as Joseph Wayne. *The Violent Land* (1954), *The Lone Deputy* (1957), *The Bitter Night* (1961), and *Riders of the Sundowns* (1997) are among the finest of the Overholser titles. *Bunch Grass* (1955) and *Land of Promises* (1962) are among the best Joseph Wayne titles, and *Law Man* (1953) is a most rewarding novel under the Lee Leighton pseudonym. Overholser's Western novels, whatever the byline, are based on a solid knowledge of the history and customs of the 19th-Century West, particularly when set in his two favorite Western states, Oregon and Colorado. Many of his novels are first-person narratives, a technique that tends to bring an added dimension of vividness to the frontier experiences of his narrators and frequently, as in *Cast a Long Shadow* (1957), filmed as *Cast a Long Shadow* (United Artists, 1959), the female characters one encounters are among the most memorable. He wrote his numerous novels with a consistent skill and an uncommon sensitivity to the depths of human character. Almost invariably, his stories weave a spell of their own with their scenes and images of social and economic forces often in conflict, and the diverse ways of life and personalities that made the American Western frontier so unique a time and place in human history.

Books are produced in the United States using U.S.-based materials

Books are printed using a revolutionary new process called THINKtech™ that lowers energy usage by 70% and increases overall quality

Books are durable and flexible because of Smyth-sewing

Paper is sourced using environmentally responsible foresting methods and the paper is acid-free

Center Point Large Print
600 Brooks Road / PO Box 1
Thorndike, ME 04986-0001 USA

(207) 568-3717

US & Canada:
1 800 929-9108
www.centerpointlargeprint.com